ESCAPED ENERGY

Written by
Jasper Quince

ESCAPED ENERGY
By Jasper Quince

Copyright 2020 Jasper Quince

I would like to dedicate this book to my grandmother,
Florence Merola, who showed me what a happy life could be. She
always made sure I was reading a book.
Through me she lives on.

Contents

Lusus Naturae

Evanescing eyes inevitably seal
And solidify behind tender flesh of the past.

Rare, blinding, these anxious nights where,
Beneath the damp sheets,
I am some Snook Monster-
Dwelling over my last meal an eternity ago.

At last, a glint,
Swimming in silence until I'm hooked,
And heaved up from the blankets.
To hang out the window.

I am
Moon-soaked,
Nude, huffing, silent.
I wear my crumbling festoon of dried memories,
Howling like the Steppenwolf within,
My grisly claws splay my eyelids
From sealing and solidifying.

Lusum Naturum.

My Handheld Sunshine

The sun is in my hands.
Solar honey-drips fill the lines of my palms,
Readings from data packed into the light that makes this, that, and all.
I take an ardent bite and pop its tender armor.

So delicious, I chomp away with strokes of passion,
Careful not to make contact with its molten pit.
I am starved of the creative juice that transforms lemons into nectarines.

The in-betweens of my teeth gather the sun's squishy,
Stringy quills,
But I would rather grin and show the world,
I am a mess, but a beautiful one.

When the sun has been picked clean,
The burn in my stomach gives me my next course of action,
I reach for a sugar cookie.

There Is a Lot of Work to be Done

So long ago we were but an unknowing seed in the dirt.

Today,

We are our own stems,
Leaves, and branches leading to something immense.

Tomorrow,

May be the same, and the day after, or even on.
Still figuring why, how, and when.

But someday,

We will be somebody's flowers.
With flowers birth seeds.

And we will have a world of interconnecting roots
To savor the amity buried in us all.

Blind Discovery; Perception

Took a ride in the rain today, crossed an overflowing river,
But it carried me away, to somewhere blissfully better.
Got stuck in the whirlpool created by elder fallen lumber.
And saw a black lobster- like creature surface from the water.

I was hoping to find reason behind,
The counteracting mothers who nurture my time,
But the monster pushed the tree to land,
And I went on and on and on.

Eventually, dumped me in a bog, and there I bobbed.
All day long, I thought, and listened to the croaking frogs.
A rolling fog came by and wept while I sipped on dark coffee.
We talked about our lives, where we'd be eventually.
When it was time to go, the fog carried on, a little brighter
And I wanted to, too, but-

Sometimes when you're stuck in a soft spot,
It's easy to fall asleep at the wheel,
It's hard to tell what's real,
So I let the greatest mother take care of me.

Jasper Quince

I had a still-water dream, of a golden-skinned, slender woman,
With weeping willow leaves for hair, and eyes as dark and soft as soil,
She held my face, her lips said nothing,
but she told me everything I should know,
A certainty anytime I needed guidance, when I felt alone,
She'll be waiting for me, as long as I make it to her.

Took a ride in the rain today, crossed an overflowing river,
And I went on and on and on.

Falling Asleep to the Sound of Rain, Again

The Unconscious lies
In a bed of feathers…
There is no ink,
No blood that can trace back
This stamp of a feeling, just a whim that finally comes,
Or just passes.
There is no fear; a human's curse,
Though, an instinctual tool to its survival.

The bed of feathers simply

S.t..r…e….t….c…h..e.S
Into a tossing sea,
Where varied shades of yellow
Beaks coast along like shark fins,
Waiting for the glint of
Emerald dragonflies hovering
Just within reach.
The Unconscious floats on.

There is no hope, or woe,
Only close or apart.

Jasper Quince

A warm, blinking, orange glow,
Like a fly during caution on the glass
Of a traffic light.
There is a rhythm.
A pattern understood,
But to The Unconscious,
It's hypnotic, however, it's…
At a level just beyond reach.

Clouds of blood.......................................Clouds of ink
On the left ....On the right

Glide from the horizon and
((((((((((((((((Combine))))))))))))))))))))
Above The Unconscious.

The sea of feathers buckles under
The stamp of a feeling
The red mixed rain brings,
And the dreamer regains conscious
From the sound of thunder.

The Freest Feeling

In transit, a seagull squawks above.
My eyes rise to the occasion.
But it is what the seagull squawks about,
That catches my ball of attention;
The freest feeling floating along.

An indigo balloon wiggles up
Through a crisp sky of azure,
A forest of clouds burst from the horizon,
Topped off with a drizzle of golden sun honey.

Everyone around wonders why,
I stare blankly at the sky,
Their thoughts direct to trouble,
Pessimism, the acid rain,

But no-

I recognize the freest feeling
As the balloon climbs so high,
Nothing can stop its dazzling reflection,
From twinkling with the stars.

A little further in the distance,
A second balloon tosses and
Flips around like a fish to catch up,
Just as free and just as beautiful.

What a strange coincidence,
But the freest feeling never travels alone.

Zephyr

Our lives are zephyrs
In hot summers of love,
Not just to exist,
But each with this unique, determined purpose.
All the while,
We combat, kiss, kill, care.
We are savages, hostiles, heroes, the hope, servants, kings & queens,
We are peace and we are war.

But at first,
We are whatever,
Satisfied in any direction,
Coerced by gusts and mother birds,
To formulate our own purpose,
Where we grow into our ambitions,
And eventually, restless-
Mind, body, soul
From within,
With a trinity of agreed certainty,
Will leap to the tip of the tongue,
Like a gold finch's first flight into the serene,
To drizzle fantastic colors beyond rainbows over
The torpid hues of a day in the life,

Over others lost in the dark,
Or withheld by excess of light,
Or stuck in the grey,
Ones who haven't tasted a breath of fresh air in ages,
And for that, they have gone mad.

Everyone is healing from something, none are unscathed
From this life worth living.

Cold Creek Memories; So Warm Now

In a cold creek, we let it fly,
Then we reel it in.
In a scraped up aluminum canoe, comfy enough for just us,
My best friend and I fish for pumpkin seeds,
Primped in fading, orange life vests,
with our bucket hats like real men,
Dreaming of snagging a big mouth bass,
But surely it was always a myth.

It is these days, when the sun crinkles its nose,
Pulls the clouds in front of it,
And leaves for a cigarette.
And yet, that thought would never
Brush the finite layers of an innocent me
In this canoe.
Instead, I'm drinking the fancy old soda pop,
Reveling in the cartoon I watched last night.

Remembering this now, I taint it, dilute or pollute it,
Until the creek is murky,
The sun hasn't returned,
And there are no fish to be found.

Then why am I fond of this memory?
Sometimes, it takes more than just remembering to bring it all back.

From the distance, in shedding cattails, and tall shrubbery,
As the canoe grinds against the rolling stones underneath,
A white stallion, its nose dipped in black, breaches from the forest
And gallops across the field.

When the horse has become aware of distant eyes,
It freezes, lifts its heavy front, dirt caked hooves,
And bucks into the sky,
Like a wolf at full moon.
Then just like it came, it left,
Me wordless, until now
When I relived the memory.

IX

Where the line stops, I step on over,
And feel the world fall from my shoulders.

I've taken my sorrows and turned them to stone,
And built out of them a home, I call my own.
I've now made a deal to let the ceiling fall.
I held it up until I couldn't bear the weight of it all.

Those who wait along the line, will wait through their many lives,
Those who are bold to cross and bear the pain are given a surprise.
Where the courage birthed from, a thousand woes,
And the story begins, a growth from the shadows.

I plan to leave a trail behind,
I plant my seeds to give back to this life,
I will not wait with the others, I will not follow,
And let another life go by that's hard to swallow.

Through the rubble, a house that once was,
I find my greatest moment, a feeling,
A key to fill the hole in my heart,
I unlock the greatest purpose, to love
Without expecting anything in return,
Even to be loved.

Impossible, Precious Foresight

Citrine summers veil the brewing doom,
Hatchets of happiness plug an opened wound.
There's a king in his castle and he chants my cursed name,
I am his soldier about to fight a battle upon his blessed plain.

By spade and stick, I have hollowed the ground into a hideout,
To save my family from the invasion because I've had my doubt,
Call it impossible, precious foresight, a king's gamble wins or dies in vain,
While the stooges who do the dirty work lose their comrades or their brains.
Sapphire and sweet, his queen stills his heart, though anxious and merry.
Antiquated as royalty can be, she must be just as ready,
Fore' if the castle bows as wilts a flower,
Her family will lose their crest and the enemy will assume its power.

When the battle unfolds in war cries, I have retreated underground.
The enemy's thunderous stomping, can only mean the end is just around.
If there's a way out, it's back to where I began,
Under rule of a new king, as a soldier for whatever he believes in.

It's a political wheel, spinning fervently to the left then to the right,
When all we need is to be steady. No more fights.
When the fields are lush emerald from the sodden blood of the dead,
Will we finally find the peace or eventually water the ground again?

Seasonal Memories for Nana; She Stays Eternal, Though Rests for Now

Spring, the Daffodils bloom first, always.
It rains, then floods. Unconditional love to all.
Soaked, I bring her a bullfrog in a box.
She releases the catch when I am not looking
And exclaims, "The frog got away!"

Summer, her garden grows wildly
With zucchini, pumpkins, asparagus...
Her and I take turns mowing the acre of lawn
For Saturday family get-togethers.
On those sweltering days, us grandchildren,
Run through the sprinkler, catching bumblebees,
While listening to the adult's purple laughter.
I can see her grilling on the deck,
Even when everyone was full, forever smiling.

Autumn, we harvest rhubarb and raspberries
From the outskirts of the encapsulating woods.
I climb to pick golden apples, pears, & plums

Jasper Quince

From her own grown fruit trees.
She is bundled in a worn, woolen sweater
Knitted from her own hands.
At night she makes one for you or me
Rocking away in her fluffy recliner, napping through reruns.

Winter, Nana wanders into a blizzard
To spread salt on ice for the family get- togethers.
Inside with a mug of hot chocolate,
I decorate her home, hanging traditions
That are as old as Nana's nana.
She sings along to timeless Christmas tapes.

This is where magic is real,
And magic will always stay,
Though rests for now.

Do Not Worry

Hard, reflecting bronze eyes
That have seen for so long, the greatest
And least memorable moments, like a
Stack of newspapers 83 years tall.

83 years has caught up.
A yarn of time sewn in & around
The heart valves of a beautiful life,
Narrowly closed, but do not worry.

Age births, grows, ripens, and rots,
The casing that preserves our souls
Accepted as fate, but fickle,
A decision must be reached in full agreement.

Between the odds of death
Sitting with her feet up,
Lies the 83-year-old whisper of hope,
Or as I'd like to call her,
The strongest woman ever.

And yet she cannot lift a finger,
Even though there's a golden will to breathe after the last breath.

Le(t)gos

I unloaded my blocks of thoughts,
Like the barrel of Legos I used to have.

Out came my nana,
With it, unconditional love,
Out came my father,
With it, unconditional pain.

I took a step back and cut my heel on a memory of running away,
When the aura of home was peevish and fatherly forceful.
So I sat in the mess, all the colors, shapes, and reasons.
Sorting without instructions, bleeding, but in abstraction.

I cried like all the times I had before, but then
I laughed like all the times I had before.
How much I'd hidden behind these toys of sorrow.
Once I proudly built a windmill, six feet high,
And my Nana was so proud. My father knocked it down.

When I cleaned my wound and scooped those Legos back in,
I decided there was no need to go through all of that again.
I let go. To let someone
Just as helpless build from the scattered,
To find that temporary protection
Only these Legos could supply for me.

The Opaque Wolf

There are wolves unseen that wander the skies of Salem,
On those wet days, hidden within the pall
Of a vanishing ghost city; one opaque wolf circles close by
Picking up the hint of blood from someone foolish or needy.

Underneath, Atlas pushes through a dense fog, on his way to work.

Life in the grey. Held like a hug.
It begins to sprinkle, the stench of the streets ascends.

A comforting silence, albeit
The beat of clicks and clacks,
His shoes, drums on the choppy brick laid path,
Thrumming through crushed cigarette packs,
Needles, tears of liquor bottles, a mangled shoe.
But Atlas is wary something is watching beyond the fog.

He looks over his shoulder, and then to the left.
The haze swiftly draws back
Revealing a black and forlorn Victorian townhouse
Stitched up in Boston Ivy.

Jasper Quince

Perched atop the cracking granite steps-
She isn't more than nine,
A child in a moment, a wolf somehow as well,
Persuades his direction, and sprinkles evolve into pouring rain.

Her knotted hair continuously splits, sparks, and fuses
Into dozens of snaking, fat, black coils.
Her hands waver in the air like flowers bending in the whirlwind.
Her eyes-
Inwardly picking up the needles from the street and
Injecting raw, apprehending rancor,
Into Atlas' recoiling blood vessels,
Rendering him thoughtless, he floats to her as prey.

Her thunderous cackles join like company,
Revealing jagged canines, crusted mustard and fragmented.
She lashes out, cupping his chin.
I just wanna bite....
Her lips retract, and out grows fur.
Saliva builds, froths, and spills out from between her fangs-
Whiskers-
Paws-

She speaks in tongues from deep down her throat,
I'll take you for my pack,
The wolf is in you, let me give you
Something you cannot give back.

Escaped Energy

Without a word, a precious thought, paralyzed,
Atlas couldn't decide if work was worth the bother,
Or living here forever, having found this matron from the ether.

The nimbostratus wolf's eyes grow wide-
Let the rain take this world away, and replace the blood with absence,
So the pain can go away.
She plunges in for a mouthwatering bite,

But some are chosen for bigger pictures,
A ward the darkness cannot crack open.
Above, the clouds fold back and the sun attacks.

The wolf retreats and its skin begins to bubble like asphalt.
Intensity, Atlas reclaims his conscious, and pushes it away.
It moans and melds into the girl, and descends into a puddle,
Trying everything to grab a nibble of flesh.

But the rain slows, then ceases.
The sun glares through thinning clouds.
The storms drift past the harbor and out to the sea.
She releases one last wail, boring into the sky.

There are wolves unseen that wander the skies of Salem,
There are guardians who put these maligned spirits
Back in their place,
So the helpless may walk the streets in peace.

⁓

No Title: i

I am a lucid bubble,
Created from a regal, oak-wood wand,
Dipped in enigmatic magic
And given a life
Not just to float away.

I've been immersed by knightly soap,
To enter the expanse above
Past the wolves circling the skies
Until I'm bathed in blue, too.

I want to journey to the big yellow bubble,
Beyond that blue and into the black,
That makes me glint of metallic violet.

But I must keep what gave me purpose safe;
Wrapped around the breath of the little girl that made me.

But when I am almost there,
A gust of wind that could de-root trees from the ground,
Shakes me up,
Throws me aside,
Pops me,

Releases my precious cargo
And I exist no longer.

History makes everything so important seem like nothing at all.
And then again, history is nothing at all.

Luxury – 1:09 A.M.

A dense fog/ rain mix pummels the pavement and creeps down the
Street.
What a luxury, sea breeze, dark air, coastal silence.
Water gathers on the sill and cascades down the grey walls; the window
Is open.
I'm drenched from this breather.
But I could complacently droop here
Forever.

Madcap Miseries

It is raining lemon juice, and everything burns.
The cities are melting or rusting- it doesn't really matter.
I hold my glass of gin like the Statue of Liberty bears her torch.
Ode To Joy, acid shower, we hide from your splash,
If we cannot find the truth, we're madcaps in the ash.

Storm of the Century

Tall and looming pines sway in circles like
Seaweed amongst the pulling, pushing, PULLING tide,
Ready to *snap*-
And lunge through the rooftop or burst through the window,
Their parting words,
You're the fool for staying. I didn't have a choice to escape.

Ravenous winds roar like hungry mountain lions,
The stomach of the beast scouring soil for some food,
But it doesn't know what. So it throws my grill across the lawn.
Fortunately, this storm isn't smart enough to backtrack.

At 2 a.m. nothing sleeps, poised and ready,
It is misty, light, and everything is hazy.
I watch a low gathering of clouds, darker than night,
Float on like zeppelins, observing the battlefield,
Bombing the area as,
The storm of the century comes to blitzkrieg us all.

How do you attack something that lacks a heart?
Prevail over something without flesh to grab?
We all wait for this Thunderbird, Demon or God to spin off somewhere else,
Asking it never finds a home, the wanderlust-ed storm.

But the weak will always perish,

The smart will survive,

The strong will be outnumbered,

The ones who run and hide will always win.

The Wondering Soul

From dawn to dusk,
The children throw stones
So high in the sky,
They never come back.

The evening settles,
Life, below as above- as pond water,
The children lay to rest,
To throw again tomorrow.

It is now, the moon appears.
Barely a sliver,
Like a worm bent in a glass jar.

Charcoal chunks, shades of black
Creep down the sky,
To the mauve horizon,
Effacing golden clouds,
The sun's guiding light,

The dark Cowles Mountain, trees, and I,
Slowly disappear.

Jasper Quince

But I'm still here,
Drinking hot coffee,
Tearing pieces off crumbly,
Red velvet cookies.

At night, the adults come out to play,
But I stare into the white worm,
And it points out all that glitters in the night.
It is only a harmless thought,
But the mauve ring constricts
My wondering soul,
Ignited like embers that will never die.
I want a silver sickle to cut myself free.
Or unsheathe the moon

And erase the Earth's blood,
That has settled to the bottom.

A Library of Knights and Nightmares

While having another cold one,
I played Sketches of Spain so loudly a memory fell off the shelf
From my library of knights and nightmares,
Landing open, sliding out, an insert of my life.
So I took the wax for a spin,
And revolved into a flashback.

A jalapeño summer day,
I lay on the roof of my maroon 88' Pontiac Safari,
The steel burns my naked back, but it makes me feel alive.
My eyes gaze into the polarized azure.
Vivid green Maples waver along the humid winds,
Soaring hawks saturate from their paradise in the sky,
where I have found mine, as well.

But I am shackled to a gourmet deli,
Enjoying the last minutes of lunch freedom,
The boss waits for my return, a short stocked, paranoid,
Lacing up his Fascist boots, while glued to his surveillance,
Watching me from the inside.

When I return from snacking on summer sun,
He senses my lifted mood, and cuts me down like a forest,

Jasper Quince

Shreds me into parliament,
And with a pen, he scratches his vented ire
That digs deeper than any cut,
As the cook cackles from behind.

The needle had been dragging around the center of Side A,
And I dared to flip it, and go down another memory alleyway.
It was the final moments I lived in Salem,
Having lost the battle to keep independence.

Alone in a house that had initially four beds,
Three friends separated and left me
With a house full of odds and ends.
Down and up three stories,
I carried everything they had abandoned,
Clothes, furniture, toys, and trash,
I was
The last fool, the last knight,
They never bothered to apologize,
This song is a sad one, The Blues played on saxophone.

I lost everything when they all gave up.
But if I hadn't gone through this pain,
I wouldn't be the knight I am now.

Some records, you just have to be in the mood for,
I slipped the wax back in its insert, and put it back in the library.
And there it is collecting dust, until I read this poem again.

The Man Alone and His Cobblestone Road

Many times, I've lost a friend, and many nights I've cried,
Pulling petals from daisies just to let myself know I tried.
I've burned a lot flower stems to bring flame to a candle,
So I can see the past's picture, though it's one that's hard to handle.

And still I can't sleep until, the slow, heavy rain,
Has hit the rooftop, and carried sounds, that help me drift away.

I've walked on many cobbled roads, and maybe hitched a ride,
But still and will I walk along until I've aged and died,
All my life I've been right home, with hopes of friends to share,
Some have joined, temporarily, now they travel roads of theirs.

And still I can't sleep until, the slow, heavy rain,
Has hit the rooftop, and carried sounds that help me drift away.

I think about the things I've done, and wonder if I've tried,
If there was something, I could have done, to stop the teary goodbyes.
But the golden rule I've learned from life, is people come and go,

I can only hope our paths cross again,
Someday,
While I walk with flowers in my hands along the cobbled roads.

Still I can't sleep until, that solemn, heavy rain,
Has hit the rooftop, and carried sounds that help me drift away.

Apocolypto

(Ringing through my ears)

The deadened white noise, day's silent cry,
A glum orange glow swallows the horizon, sun, and sky.
The air is virulent, ground is tarnished
And everyone alive was incessantly admonished;
Now everyone alive is left to die.

(Some people anticipated for this to happen,)

Before the great Nuke kissed Mother Earth,
Stockpiling artillery, canned goods, and narcotics with mirth.
They hid in their premeditated bunkers,
Survivors apprehensively refer to them as Marauders.
Starving sharks, crimson lips, greedy grins arising to this new birth,

(Denouncing the breath of life, the last hope for mankind.)

And when I lay in fear at night,
Nothing again will be okay,
The Earth is a festering blight
As we all slowly decay.

Jasper Quince

(I'm better than this world today, but not better off)

Yellowed waves of the radiated Atlantic crash upon a nearby reef,
The sand has rusted bronze, ashes flutter in the air,
And decomposing carcasses of aquatic animals jut from beneath,
The smell of sulfur is pungent as my watery eyes hesitate,
Offshore, a lonely tree, however bearing no leaves.

At a nose's length away,
Scratched into the bark,
"Always move, never linger."
Then I see the severity, blood-drunken Marauders.
I stifle and back away from foul play.

A barely discernible body,
Hand's tied behind, tied to the stump's other side.
She must have clawed the writing, before she slowly died.
I cannot look for long, I must go, most assuredly,
And so I get back to the road and forget the tree in a hurry.

There once was a time, you'd never guess,
When the sun rose and the moon slept,
The air was pure,
People smiled when they wept.

And now, when I lay to rest at night,
Nothing again will be okay,
The Earth is a festering blight.
As we all slowly pray.

Hideaway on West Center Road

In twilight's favored moment,
Where the black forest barely stirs,
Amongst the wolves that howl in hunger,
Endures the remains of a chapel that burned down 200 years ago;
A marble alter, a slab wall, and a story,
The sheen of dew shimmers on moss in moon glow.

In a neighboring field, crooked tombstones
Jut up from the ground,
As if the victims eternally try to escape the flames.

These tablets bear worn out names,
Preserved by ancient lore,
And local ancestors who visit to lay flowers and flags.

And behind it all, those tightly knit, rampant woods
Spread up a rounded mountain,
Where brown bears graze on blackberries,
And rusted car skeletons lay buried in decomposition,
Providing shelters for wasps and field mice.

And out of the random,
I recall these gurgling streams that ran like veins

Jasper Quince

Into deposits where beavers assembled their dams.
These secret lands, where stone trails were built,
By Union Soldiers in the Civil War,
Where I'd walk alone in youthful contemplation.

The church is a stop on the curving road,
Where "country driving" happens,
Where wild turkeys and red foxes meander across,
Where the world has been touched gently,
Over the period of humans.
It is here, I've locked away a peace that echoes
When I need it the most.

It is here, my bare feet squash the soft grass
In search of pinhead wild strawberries,
In search of connecting a beautiful, but melancholy past,
With a beautiful, meaningful present.

The Ja(ded)Gu(llible)Ar(chetype)

The wheels spin in stillness,
Burning rubber like butter.
The worn out door of opportunity is momentarily open,
The Jaguar, steps into a stranger's car.

The sun has closed an archetypical eye,
While the moon hangs out, plump, ready to fall.
It took a slice of lemon on the lip,
To notice the sting of endangerment.

Oh, habits, those clustery, bumps on the skin
No one is supposed to know about. Oh, Jaguar, I'm so sorry.

The slandered warlock of expiry will soon figure out,
It has all bloodlines, elder and infant in its grasp.
For now, it has chosen you,
Buzzing around this car, thrashing on the windows,
While the jungle on fire fervently watches from afar.

Oh, foul, what love coils behind naked eyes?
Oh Jaguar,
What lack of being seen will make you but a fable to the future.

The Woman Who Collected
Rain Drops

It was the end of another arduous shift at The Spirit Bookstore in Marblehead.
Atlas wound down the black & white awnings, balanced the drawers,
And added leftover money to the Presidential Fund, used to buy more books.
The brick sidewalks always led him back to Salem and eventually, home.

During late afternoons when the sun descended to such a degree
That it knocked over its can of paint,
And its secret stash of golden oils spilled all over the sky,
He would take a detour, to an abandoned building,
Up a fire escape, and relax on the rooftop,
Where the view was worth the toll of the day,

Crippled brake lines, his Safari Wagon had given up,
Which coerced Atlas to hike six miles to and back from The Spirit
Five days a week.
His motive was the threat of eviction,
Roommates who disappeared on Christmas,
So he struggled to pay rent for their absence.
Little could bring him joy during these physically demanding days,
But the Northshore sunset setting over the Atlantic Ocean-
It was going to be another perfect one for the ages.

Escaped Energy

Atlas slipped into the building from the back.
As soon as he shut the fire exit door behind him,
The walls shuddered like beaten snare drums,
Shaking dust and dirt from the ceiling.

Rattled, he tried to push the door back open,
But it would not budge. He tried again. Accepted he was trapped.
Instead of getting compacted by this building's downfall,
He thought he could call from the roof to a person passing by,
And maybe they'd open the door for him. He went up,
Even though the stairs wobbled, and the railing dislodged from the wall.
He began to notice the walls didn't just throb, but resembled a heartbeat.
Water started to trickle through cracks at an alarming rate.

When he reached the top, a tall, brass-pointed umbrella rested parallel to
The last step.
The building's tremors paused, but the water only intensified.
He looked down and saw that the entire first floor was submerged.
He picked the umbrella up and opened the door.

Fresh air filled his lungs with relief, temporarily.
The wind whipped Atlas' skin like dragging tiny fangs,
Raindrops fat and heavy plopped into puddles already formed on the roof.
The clouds lit up like an overabundance of fireworks,
Flashing through a fog that looked like a pack of wolves running circles,
The smell of electricity stung his nostrils, and wet his eyes.

At the edge,
Where he usually watched the sunset,

40

Amidst showers and shadows, a stranger in a raincoat,
Tirelessly picked up aluminum coffee cans strewn in clusters,
And tossed them over the edge.

Atlas tightly grabbed the rusted railing that encompassed the edge.
Pushing through the intense storm, he stumbled forward,
Shouting through his other arm, this building was going to fall.
But the stranger ignored his presence and continued to do their service.
Dozens of cans were scattered everywhere, collecting rain.
And when they filled,
The stranger picked them up, and gleefully watched them
Plummet into the city's abyss.

The closer Atlas got, the more he noticed
Very long, silvery hair thrashing in the wind.
The stranger's face peaked out like a slice of the moon,
Her eyes stayed down but they strangely were
Illuminated like crystals in the sun,
She was beautiful. She was collecting rain drops.

The next can she reached for, he let go of the railing,
Dashed over to kick it aside.
The woman's eyes flickered like flags in the wind,
But with so many stars, possibly planets, twinkling in them,
She withdrew in her coat, and pulled the hood tighter,
Then searched for the next can.

Atlas asked if the umbrella he found was hers.
And it was, but she did not say, just nodded.

She glided over to get it.
Instead, she deftly grabbed his wrist. She pulled her arms to her chest,
Pulled his body close, they both rose up from a geyser,
And brushed his lips with hers,
Forgotten, the wicked & splintered storm; reality.

The woman was surreal; a complexion Atlas instantly fell in love with.
She leaned back and pulled his hands,
And he complied in a sudden understanding he was safe.

The railing grew soft, and snapped,
Growing from the ends, over the edge
Winding down the side of the building as
Vines, leaves sprouting at a thrilling rate.
Moss formed from the puddles, so dense, it was spongy to step on,
They reached near the edge, both looking onward,
As if ready to take a step onto the crackling black clouds.

Atlas became encumbered under the spell of vertigo,
And recoiled from her perfect touch.

A pop of lightning struck the side of the building.
Glass flung out, along with cement, and burning insulation,
The surface trembled, tilting their axis, cans tipped and washed away,
The umbrella, too. The two tumbled on the moss,
And the water escaped over the edge like a waterfall,
The vines quickly grew to sew the damage, but could only hold up the roof.
Over the edge, he could hear the chomping of teeth, but could see only grey.

Atlas crawled over like a crab, reaching
A leg on cement, a leg on spongy turf.

He looked back to see his earthly angel had risen to her feet,
The edge slipped and sloped, straining to hold on.
A fissure grew between them,
Exclaimed awareness was in her eyes.
She yearned to be on his side,
Though fatal, Atlas yearned to be on hers.

He gathered the strength to jump over the growing crack,
But took a moment to come to a realization, his future
Belonged to his current side. He could not dismiss it.
On that other side he stood up, held out his hands, and pleaded,
Come home with me.

Looking down she shook her head, but smiled the best she could.
An empty can rolled by, and Atlas snatched it up,
Rainfall filled it fast, and he lunged out to put it in her hands.
Reluctantly, it was what she wanted, even if it was extra weight.

The crevice spread further and pushed off the building's wall,
Atlas watched in horror, as the moss, the vines, and the cans
Were swallowed in the black underbelly of the starving night
Along with the woman who collected rain drops.

His knees connected with concrete, and he bellowed like a malaise viola.
From the blackness, the umbrella, open, glided up and landed in front of him,
It was the first time he noticed the drop patterns on it.

Escaped Energy

So he took it, feeling a gentle breeze feather his body.

As he opened the door back to the inside world,
Something in his heartbeat felt familiar,
It remained warm and full, as if it had let someone new move in,
And he knew there would be another time,
Another place, where they would meet again,
Somewhere far enough to call it an adventure,
Hopefully watching a beautiful sunset.

The door closed behind him,
On the first step was an aluminum can full of
Silvery reflecting water.
Atlas picked it up and drank as if it were a goblet until it was empty.
The liquid filled his head with a special feeling
Only the rarest and luckiest people encounter
In many lifetimes.

Atlas descended the stairs, drenched and dripping,
His shoes squished with every step,
When he reached the ground floor, he opened the door-
Where the sun still poured out unto the city,
And it was going to be a beautiful sunset.
So he turned around.
Went back up to go watch it.

Asteroid Awareness

It is larger than observatories,
Slashing through The Milky Way,
Slung from the plutoid Eris,
Thirsty for a taste of *our* planet.

Like fingers pinching the flame to a candle's wick,
The Earth could disappear and join all that is black in space.

What will we do if Dysnomia crash lands?

The news outlets will tell us without time to plan,
Fear-stricken families, huddled in their basements,
Embraced to the cadence of white noise and stifled tears,
Until, there is no light
To recover our lost eyes.

This time it whizzes by, giving us the middle finger,
Knowing someday, physics will win and so will the asteroid.
When will we work together to figure this out?
Are we a species that only learns after,
Or will we evolve to figure it out ahead of time?

Dazed Days

Little rain, to scatter on the window,
When I am dazed in vain.
An eerie glow from the river that wraps around my home
Crawls like a school of snakes,
I feel Indigo.
Is it coming, staying,
Or just passing,
By?
I slip on my raincoat,
And burst out the door.
Worst so far,
A boot sopped of puddle,
And that puddle stamped with my paw.
 Close by, the river is a melted pathway of gold.
In the center, a stone black monolith juxtaposed,
Veiled in narrow weeds and perturbed snails,
The tippy top enshrouded in discolored mold.
I cannot recall all of this. I must be dreaming.
I let my legs dangle over the river's bank.
Rainbow trout flail above the surface,
And flop into the gunk from which they came.
I yank at my boot and dump out the puddle.
The river's glow becomes dark.

The rain starts to downpour.

Thunder growls like unceasing hunger.

Lightning zips through the evergreens and ignites a fiery disaster.

My hazelnut eyes glaze over. Take me away.

A string of electricity reaches the stone,

And spirals around,

The weeds and snails let go.

The rock grunts, then chortles,

Like a velvet shock.

Then slinks back to the depths below.

The boot in my hand accidently lost.

The fire calms, it never burned.

And I go back inside to sip on hot chocolate with mini marshmallows.

And the glow subsides.

Color Wheel

I need to finger-paint
Like I used to;
Go COLOR crazy.

Fire hydrants the color of public pool floors,
The scratch of cross hatch to resemble the shimmer of reflected sun,
Framed by myrtle sidewalks
That melt off the canvas.

I want to smudge faces imperfect,
With every color, paint their skin, it doesn't matter,
The details like those are petty,
And we are all evolved as equals.

Mauve clouds absconding from
A single cracked mason jar
Brimming of rose-pedaled skies.

Drench my hands in bubbling color and
Drag my knuckles through oily eyes.
Thwarting a limit until
I reluctantly add a drop or two of
Violet, milky tears to finish the picture.

No Title: ii

Trapped in blocks we've built around ourselves,
With roofs to let nothing in,
Sometimes, it's healthy to absorb the rain,
Everyone is ready for some event,
Equipped with phones, tv's, and internet
To capture, edit, and socialize their feelings.

Splayed from the sky, it rains in buckets
Of metal, fire-stricken wings, and hearts without a beat,
A churning of thick steel warping with velocity,
And thumps in the ground, like an Earth tremor.

And everyone is inside, except the ones who fear nothing.
Everyone has a hole they can stick their lazy hand through,
To take a clipping of something they're part of, but not a part of,
The comforts of being disclosed…

All the while, everyone blames everyone for making the sky fall,
Because no one could see who had done it.

An inkling makes me think the ones who want to bury the mess,
Are behind it all, but we'll never know,
Being this blind, with this much potential at our fingertips.

Love Me Syndrome

Another tempestuous night in Town Park, melancholy
Wild Thoughts, seeks harbor from the fell dampness.
Across an old Maple, restroom facilities, in a stall,
His Swiss Knife carves, *help!- a grounded cardinal,*
Over faded, besought scratches, then his number.

The windows behold an ashen canvas, dashing away
A lustrous moon, sour lampposts, the path back & ahead,
But in buckets of rain, runs a scarlet damsel his way.
Wild Thoughts escapes on some path, Love Me Syndrome
Skips past roley- poley earthworms stuck in puddles.

The gales deepen in fury. By the Maple, a scarlet,
Melancholy soul runs to the restroom, closes the stall.
She sees unspeakable markings, one freshly concerning.
A knife on the basin, she dials the splintered number,
My name is Lonesome Dove, I've waited a long time for you.

A calm develops, drenched footsteps echo anticipations.
The beautiful ones, raised to know what comes & goes,
But not what stays- saturated under fluorescent sight,
They sparkle. Lonesome Dove eases five minutes in.
Your real name isn't Wild Thoughts. Care to know mine?

Jasper Quince

From outside, a whip of lightning licks the Maple,
Crackling, thickly green branches smoke up, catch fire.
They ponder a tragic moment. *Is it you?* He knows, *It's
Me. Tragedy.* She flies, red tail vanishing in the rain.

That night, a tornado brewed, ravaging Town Park.
Love Me Syndrome claimed one, but not the other.

When a Pawn Warns Their Bishop

Their ways of understanding fill the steel basin,
As they want, not a drop more or less.
Let the stillness reflect their feelings,
Cool as floor tile, sharp as business kills.

Everyone heard about those stock market uncertainties.
The king hangs off the rung above,
Tersely slips a heating plate underneath,
Set to boil. *Bubble over, let the liquid
Take its place, rain running fire starter.*

Disguised in crystal clear, the liquid's granulated sugar water,
Fore the king charms the soldiers, peasants, and all naive.
The bishop passes down his orders, sacrifices his pawns,
And is wooed he will not be next.
Somebody please, bring a towel, this has gotten to be quite a mess.

When a pawn warns their bishop,
He can only watch the signal flare with unmoving eyes.
Cold and silent, their ways of understanding fill the basin,
But there's not enough for anyone else, but the king and his game.

This Job Isn't Big Enough for the Two of Us

Quiet down now, beautiful little bygones.
Your melancholy harmony was your greatest allure.
When I walk away like a cowboy into the sunset, you'll miss
The point, and that's something I'll have to live with.

I'll throw around words of distaste like boulders,
Looking for the golden ruling, but I'll never be able to speak my heart.
Down by the water hole, I have reflected more than a man does in a
Lifetime, And I've found just as much, because there is only one answer,

The past is Four Roses on the rocks, and after a few,
I'm drunk in memories, though it's easiest to forget.
Strangers will gather and help me sing this song,
That digs me deeper, closer to my grave.

The aces of life I laid on the table doubled its value,
But the dealer knew better and rigged the river,
And all that time wishing for the jackpot,
Left me with nothing but kindly banter from the others being played.

Yes, the fear of untimely change can make a man's paunch ache,
Biting fingernails, sleepless nights, snappy judgment, blind eyes,

Rest assured, everything will be all right.
But first things first, get through the night alive.

Today I'll ponder mortality; tomorrow I'll fight it.
And that's the answer, every time.
Today I'll drink and toast. Tomorrow I'll find a new town,
And call it my own, until it's time for my sunset again.

Dead Man's Horse

What is paler than the moon's glazed glow?
Its reflection.

They call it a desert, because it wants to be left alone,
But I ignore the angry sun and make myself at home.
I enjoy nothing here, but a few yuccas over there,
While I dig for water with a buffalo's sun decayed shoulder bone.

I ride on a dead man's horse,
Towards the black hazy heart in the sand,
Most who try to find it, will never understand,
You have to be raised like it to ask of such demand.

A dry way to survive, beats living in the city,
The ones left alone, gain the pleasure to do as they please.
Laws are fine as the grains I tread upon,
No one sees nothing, so no one sees me.

I ride on a dead man's horse,
Heading Southwest Ajo,
Running away is my only course,
Fleeing is all I know.

Fill my bags with your belongings, and ride away the night.
Once I find the blackened heart in the pale reflection of the well
I'll finally begin to see the light.

The Life (Yellow Boat Part i)

Auburn newts bask on the dock,
Thickets of cattail,
Sprout from between wooden planks
Spaced like gapped teeth.

Enshrouded,
The shadow of a hulking willow
Drapes over,
And caresses the dock,
With its fingerlike leaves,
A
Yellow boat-for-two
Follows the domesticated tug and push
Of slow waves from the gentle current,
Refreshing a stone shoreline,
And then draining it dry.

The boat peels near its edges and great curves,
But exhibits no age otherwise.

Along the sides,
Hand painted in crimson
Cursive lettering,
La Vida.

Escaped Energy

Two maple oars
Splinter in the constant heat,
Worn at the ends,
Collocated in the seat,
Like anxious dogs.

IF'S MIGHT WORK

I am The Rain Cloud,
F'loating like a lazy flounder in the deep blue
Skies.

My sojourn's reason requires
I, The Rain Cloud, to
Give my burden to a desolate,
Hot, thirsty land,
That breeds healthy life.

Word will spread, "Manna from Heaven…"
Obeisance, as the children, with their charmed
Rain sticks in little fingers,
Knight each other for their noble work of my downfall.

Nana's Television

Sometimes,
I dream of stealing the rusted axe from the garage,
To strike down that COLOR hot box.

I'd creep up those crooked stairs ,
The way crooked people do with crooked intentions,
Peaking around,
Her plush teal recliner popped back in position,
The program convincing her to stay tuned.

As she snoozes during a yarn session,
I'd simper on by and plant that cold steel head through
My Nana's television.

Nothing more than the swiftest of a slice,
Cutting the apple to see its black star,
And the T.V sputters its last juicy sparks.

Nana gasps,
"I wouldn't know what to do with myself,"
When I let her in on my daydream.
But sometimes…

Saying Goodbye Is the Hardest Part

It feels like the pearl stripped from its mother.
Tree after tree axed down when all it gave us was oxygen,
The impression of the rainbow seeped from the painter's eyes.
Saying goodbye is the hardest part.

Yet, without change, the body sticks like molasses,
Always aware, forever restless,
Yet something blocks the neurons, auto-piloting routines.
And when your zombie finally rests,
It plaques your dreams as a collage of infectious memories.

Saying goodbye makes you look at everyone differently,
If it is the last time you will see them,
You treat them with
Big eyes, a bigger heart, and the biggest tears.

We say goodbye for various reasons;
Tired of the old we desire to stray from,
To reawaken a hibernating soul
Collecting clumps of dirt and long dried leaves.

We say goodbye, sometimes, to hurt others,
To etch into the loser's mind, Hey-
I'm only human, treat me fairly,
The burden of your pain is not sharable.
I won't live forever, and so you say.

But more-so we say goodbye because we have to.
Be it good or bad, but change,
Change is the next chain link to saying goodbye,
Because saying goodbye can really be the hardest part to living.

It is the casket of the past that is buried deeply away from touch,
Like a time capsule, only, it is saying goodbye,
And if it were dug up decades from now,
All would be gone but their bones of existence.

We say goodbye to save others.
Love can keep you glued to a papery situation,
That is taut during an onward, bumpy road
That tears it again & again,
Yet taping the rips replaces drastic ideas to say goodbye.

It's saying goodbye to love,
When you pull the car aside on that bumpy road,
Because words are more powerful than headaches than hammers,
You search and find the black instead of the almond eyes of love,
They look away at the stars, and you cry
Because they are saying goodbye without words,
Your thoughts skip along the river of tears you make for love.
It's saying goodbye to love that is the hardest part.

But saying goodbye is the glass cannon of mixed results.
It could fire off perfectly, which rarely happens.
It could shatter from harsh impact, slicing open your vulnerable change,
Or, it could send you, the iron ball, rolling to the side,
Somewhere you would have never seen before
Inside that barrel.

And that chance is why saying goodbye is the hardest part,
But that chance is why,
Why we ever say goodbye at all.

Best Friend

Beyond the fringes of somatic reality,

Awakens the ghastly remains of a memory,
Longing to reconnect,

For raison d'être, even I do not know.

Our eager minds would converge like cars through a tunnel,

And every time I was the driver, I'd crash into a wall halfway,
Thinking too hard, daydreaming…

A silent movie plays for an empty audience,
But the reel pitters and skips like rain,
Soaks the grass on the silver screen,
And, somehow, we're in it,

Blasting rainbows of sparkled stars
Into the belly of the dark and pouring sky.
They shoot up and drag their tails along,
Eventually swallowed by chalky, brooding clouds.

Jasper Quince

The reel plays matinees once in a while.
Even though our minds don't convene anymore.

Where did you go, best friend?

Lessons

When I was ten, Nana bought a pine birdhouse with a flapper for a roof and nailed it to a tree by her feeders. Identifying birds was one of her favorite hobbies and she knew them all. From Starlings, to Blue Jays, Golden Finches to Oriels, we had a plethora of species visit this sacred area. I remember one morning, Nana went outside with birdseed in her hand and a black cap chickadee landed on the tips of her fingers to have a nibble. Hanging outside was a hummingbird feeder that was changed almost daily, and a squirrel-proof feeder, the squirrels still managed to dip their paws in. It only made her laugh.

One day I saw a bird squeeze into the opening of the birdhouse. I wanted to see the bird inside so I climbed the tree and opened the flapper.

Inside was a slate- grey, Tufted Titmouse bundled in its nest guarding two eggs. As if it happened a month ago, I can remember its black, beady eyes scared to death and her beak half-open with a sliver of pink inside. I desired a closer look, though.

I wrapped my tiny hands around Mother Bird, and stole her from home. The eggs were grey and brown speckled, but shiny. Mother bird chirped in anger, but I did not put her back. Instead, I tucked her in my shirt and leapt from the tree. We then walked along the edge of the lawn where elderberries and blackberries grew. When we reached the end where the woods expanded, I showed Mother Bird my favorite place that made me happy called Leaf Heaven. Every autumn, the wind would sweep the roasted yellow, orange, and red Maple leaves from the lawn and dump them here, where piles of leaves were already made to jump in. It was summer, though, so the area was very shaded, fore the leaves were chartreuse, blocking most of the sun.

I thought this spot made her joyful as well, and I was glad to share something sincere with this little angel.

When returning Mother Bird to its nest, I took a detour around our back porch. It was cool from the July heat. The floor was made of brick and that is key because suddenly Mother Bird had enough. She bit my finger. More shocked than hurt, I threw the bird to the ground. That feeling, *What have I done,* surged through my veins.

I quickly picked it up. A driblet of blood spewed from its mouth. It did not chirp, and its beady eyes asked me why. I ran to the birdhouse, climbed the tree, and placed her back on top of its eggs, hoping I had not killed all three. I felt so sad, I cried all afternoon in my room.

Anxiety had gotten the best of me. I had to check a day later, hoping the bird was healing. The bird was dead.

Never again did a family of birds live in that birdhouse.

I checked again a week later to help the baby birds I hope had hatched. The birdhouse was empty, and I pretended to not know why. Year after year, Nana checked. And never did I tell her what happened.

From that day, I learned important lessons that helped structure who I am today. I vowed never to kill any living animal and love everything for what they are. And to this day, I'd like to think animals understand me better than humans ever will.

When I was older, I'd find abandoned baby birds that had fallen from their nests. Mother birds will not save them if this happens. I'd take them in and keep them, flipping rocks for worms and feeding these poor saps I felt akin to. They never survived, but at least I tried.

No Title: iii

It is late on a Sunday night,
The wolves howl, my stomach, too.
My pen is between limbo,
And my fingers scramble my blabbering thoughts,

I constantly seek new words,
In dire hope of finding the perfect one for the occasion,
A word to end my worries, pay my rent,
Show me love, raise my vibration.

There is a definition for anything that can be thought.
You just have to find the right language.

Ever since I was young, I loved the tongues,
The new ways to roll my r's in Spanish,
To pronounce my v's as w's in Latin,
Tashkils used to give vowel recognition between
Every letter in Arabic, but I never became fluent in any language.

Finishing projects is a sinking ship for me,
I let some of them flee to the life boats, and
Others I force to drown with me.
My ship is complicated for others to understand,

Escaped Energy

Sometimes it turns into a submarine,
And we all survive.

It was difficult growing up as I did.
Without, a mother to cook soul food,
Without a father to guide my growth.

I was just a boy,
Who did not understand
 Why they locked themselves away for hours,
While the dirty clothes piled high,
And I fed the cat as well as myself.
Why we would go on adventures
To meet strange people
To give away those dirty clothes in a trash bag
And all I had to wear was a pair of overalls over my bare skin.

I could not understand why my father and mother split up,
The roaring rage of my father and his blue Subaru,
As he screamed, out the window at my mother.
Even I did not know what it meant, but I knew it hurt.
Her moaning, crumpled on the couch
And I could not get through to ease the burden,
So I carried it.

It is difficult knowing you're different,
And different knowing I am difficult.
An individual learner.

Jasper Quince

It is late on a Sunday night,

Even the wolves have ceased to howl,

My pen still in limbo,

And my fingers burn from writing my blabbering thoughts.

⁘

It is an eerie night on the Northshore.
The Boston Celtic's lead quickly dwindles in the final quarter.
Winds are picking up, thunder echoes,
As darkness looms over like a black lamppost,

Throwing January Gill O'Neill off her "Kandy Shoes."
Breathing anvils and anchors, Poet Michael Weaver
Reads "Tunafish"
To dry a soaked, dedicated crowd of academics,
While lost in memories of
Erotic secrets he and Lucille Clifton exchanged.

I have never felt an evil like this,
Did the marrow in my bones freeze?

The Celtics just lost by 20 points
And the rain pummels the roads like a war drum.

"These winds have never made my windows rattle so hard,"
Larry, the neighbor says, rolling cigarettes to ease the stress.
Living in this apartment building for 16 years,
I can tell even he is timid,
As the ambulances wail on by.

Fire trucks too,
Spurting layers of sludge water that slap the windows
And I am so goddamn cold.

Creaks I have never heard, down the hall,
Something with low batteries cackles?
Tenants slamming doors.
Where do they need to go in this weather?

It is a haunting night on the Northshore.
U.S. Olympic Nordic Trekkers won gold and silver today.
This ditch of disaster isn't affecting the rest of the world,
Or even the U.S. for that matter.

"If my T.V. loses power tonight I'm going to kill somebody,"
My neighbor spits through his teeth.

In my living room, I light my only candle.
For some reason it burns so dimly.
The front doorknob jiggles and
I want to break out in tears of apprehension.

Through the silence of the flickering light,
I hear my neighbor Fred
Riding his obnoxiously noisy scooter home.
I can imagine his face in disgust,
As the rain pelts his coat,
Drenches his jeans,
Leaks inside his helmet and up his nostrils.

His vrrrooooooomm… is hastened tonight, then cut short.
Run for your life, Fred.

How long will the power be out for?
The ambulances continue to howl,

Across the street the manager at the 7-11
Gobbles down chocolate bars, in the dark,
Smoking Marlboro Reds,
Locked inside his glass doors, grinning in hysteria.

Rumors say we are flooding.
"Northshore the New Atlantis!"
I can see the headliners tomorrow, if we make it.

I hear my neighbor Fred
Riding his obnoxiously noisy scooter home,
His vrrrooooooomm… is hastened tonight, then cut short....
Wait I already heard that.

Did I mention I feel so goddamn cold?
"If my T.V. loses power tonight, I'm going to kill somebody."
Run for your life.

The Night I lost My Sanity

Suicide Cabin

Forsaken,
Tucked in the depths of
Berkshire evergreen mountains,
Condoned as a grave,

A forlorn hunter blasted himself
And bled his intentions into the floorboards.
The story piques my interest
And I wrangle a team to investigate.

We hike for two miles.
There is no sign of life,
Replaced by bear traps and barbed wire
So we tread slowly.

A rusted ladder is propped against a Pine,
Its lower branches stripped away,
Small studded handles,
Climb up to a rotten plywood platform.

Just below, a bone-yard
A dark aura,
A jigsaw,
A feeling to flee.

Scattering the ground are 12 gauge shells of yellow and red,
Bronzed caps now a sea-foam green.
I pick one up and picture a deer with holes, writhing right here.
Dirt clods and gunpowder spill onto my hands.
We eventually reach Suicide Cabin,
Moose brown, the wood decays
Like the body inside,
Thirteen days after hikers of The Appalachian found it.

Centipedes and earwigs,
Writhe between planks,
Moths cling to the outside walls,
Spiders work to paint the house white.

Its door creaks like crickets,
Reluctantly opening,
Disturbing a mass cluster of mosquitoes.
I pick up bad intentions at the welcome mat.

Through the bug cloud,
My hands cover my head,
I duck to my knees,
As they filter out the door.

The scene is painted for me,
One room, one window,
The dried blot in the center, on the floor,
The air is hard to breath.

Pushed aside, an off-pink loveseat,
Lacking cushions,
Also stained,
Its left front leg snapped.

Did he suffer?
Did he cry?
Did he not succeed at first,
To rest in peace on this couch…

Wooden shelves that line the wall,
Coffee cans from 1970.
Smokey the Bear story books,
Porcelain animal figurines-

I pocket those.
But maybe I shouldn't have taken the essence with me.

A calendar from the current year
The death was so recent
I can feel it,
In fact, I can taste it, somehow.

On our way back home,
Our journey leads us through a neighbor's yard.
A series of barks,
From three bloodthirsty hounds.

A fence between them and us,

Their eyes, bloodshot red,

On hind legs,

They might just jump over the fence and kill us, too.

An irate hunter exits his house

And orders us to stop,

And when we do, he points his finger up, up, up.

"Whatever you do, don't go in that cabin, you hear!"

I finger the porcelain figurines in my pocket,

As we nod our heads,

And go our separate ways.

Caught in Action

Within a sprawl of palm trees varnished in Agent Orange,
I am intrigued like a monkey, peering down at
Nine moss-capped U.S. soldiers
Who are lost.

Marlboros dangle from their trembling lips,
Each face pinched permanently.
Some are burdened with scars, bruises,
Some, Bibles, but they all
Carry their own memory of Home,
That keeps them away from here, Devil's Bog.

The trees are so slippery with chemical I can't hold a firm grip,
And I slip,
Fall
On my back,
Like a helpless turtle,
Impacted into the mud.

Nine rifles,
Directly aim in the holes of my ears, nostrils,
And awaiting possibilities.
But after a moment of recognition,

An electric, grizzly bear of a man,
Lends a tattooed arm and hoists me up.
Now I'm a moss-capped soldier with a pinched face.
He then passes over a lit cigarette.
And then there were ten.

Up ahead, a trickling brook slithers through the forest.
From afar, it is out of place. And beautiful.
One soldiers stops, unfolds a tarp atop the mud,
Kneels on it, and
Sets up a field phone.

I reach the brook to satiate a sudden thirst,
But the brook is red as wine.
The other soldiers fill their canteens anyways.

Why, this river has no reflection,
I thought out loud.
I cannot see myself, and I don't know why.
It is deep, and perplexingly rapid.

Rolling along the crimson current,
Hundreds of smoldered bodies jounce at the crest of water,
Bewildered in nonsensical dimensions.
A few still wail and groan, crack, whimper.
I am overwhelmed and ill at my hands and knees.

Shells blindly drill through still air,
The endless clash of cymbals.

We are being ambushed.
Mortars from heaven rain to the ground with thunderous belches.
The duds smack into mud.

One by one we succumb to the Gods of Warfare.
Even the tattooed man who helped me before,
Disappears in a blast of smoke.
My soldiers are losing,
And all I can do is look at my boots.
I am lost.

My eyes lose the glint within.
I prop a borrowed rifle on my shoulder,
Cheek resting on the barrel,
Focused on my aim.

I see my targets in the crosshairs,
But no matter how much I concentrate, I am shot with fear.
I don't turn around, though. I fire.
Finger cemented on the trigger,
Until I'm smoking empty, but it doesn't matter.

Nuclear Bomb

I watch as the grey brain blossoms from Ground X,
Man's steel seed finally planted.
Swords of flame stab skyward.
An inferno within burns like the end of a **cigarro,**
Rooting from a twisting stone pedestal.

Then, when the vortex can no longer climb,
It hangs,
And scatters in the air like a mega firework or
A fatally attractive woman letting her hair down.

Another brain ruptures from the other.
Grow little seed, big and strong.
This one, space-bound.
It gathers a smoky blackness from the lower,
Causing the other to flare into a small sun.

The new brain builds and expels the blackness,
A thick smoke ring,
That soars along the edge of space
Erasing clouds behind blue,
And slowly
Sewing itself into the atmosphere.

Absolute

Woe, is the night,
Beneath my droopy eyes, bowls of onyx agate
Collect the swirling pools of age, stress, and loneliness. I escape
In an aluminum coffer to rove along the spines of snaking roads,
Roads that take people places, roads that bring people nowhere.

Somewhere, over the Blackberry Hills,
Somewhere where silence licks closed the envelope of anxiety,
And pushes it through the crack of the window,
My legs loosen a straining pressure applied to the gas pedal,
And I coast along the curls of concrete, until my car tenders the moment, here,
At this chapel on a hillock that burned down during a mass 200 years ago,
Leaving only an alter, and a cemetery for the unfortunate.
With guidance from the moon, I find myself
Resting atop the alter like a tablecloth.
My arms and legs dangle over the cutting marble's edges.
I watch the tiny stars shoot past-

It's time for love's structure to crumble
Like a stack of bricks atop a shuddering Earth,
It's time to peel the thick skin from the fruit of my heart
And feed its scraps to the birds,

Escaped Energy

It's time to surrender.
It's time to grow up, this moment-

Ornaments of the universe, how have I come to be...

Those were the days, we'd spread our blankets across the velvet grass,
Sharing a picnic with the ants,
Attempting to pinpoint the location of an imaginary factory in the sky
That produced and pumped out such billowy, beautiful clouds just for us.
We'd follow along the outskirts of the fields
Picking blackberries to feed them to each other,

I wait forever, until dawn's brilliant colors
Paint the sky golden, with rosy clouds.
The drive back is meaningless.
I pull over and pick up my envelope lying in the middle of the road.
And then I look in the rear view mirror
Noticing my droopy eyes have gotten lighter.

No Title: iv

In between the hands of hours, time swept under a door to the house of life,
It went somewhere untraceable, minute mice lightly breathing
Behind rooms of overlarge things, in nests of seconds comprised of
The smallest memories, not even a human could remember.

The clock struck midnight, this grand, mahogany, white-faced grandfather,
With silver tick tocks, racing for years, at an unchangeable pace.
Wound its gears through the golden years in the house of life,
Created meaning and enforced its laws, though never realizing;

Some people watched its motions and tensed up,
Thinking of being rushed,
Picturing a one on one fight, loser draws first blood today-
Some follow time like roads, and they drive on,
Never knowing where to go,
Until an accident or attraction catches an eye to pull over.

And then there are a few, who know, through clever nights, listening,
Waiting for the clocks to talk, and realizing that time answers for no one,
Because time is relatively false.
For that, they are the wisest.

Silver Sickles

Silver sickles fall like rain,
Causing damage, so much pain.
Peering through a frosty window,
I hold my tongue to thoughts…
خففي لي, (Relieve me…)

Silver sickles,
Men lay restful tucked in coffers.
Their eyes like clay,
The time has come,
To accept to forget truculent orders.

Silver sickles, decide to subside,
I pick one up on my way outside,
I grip the melting dagger
So cold and so shrill,
Looks can kill, but memories never die.

Slip into my pocket just for the thrill,
Silver sickle follow me,
Meddlesome or company we shall see.

Silver sickle guides me,
Like the graceful fingertip of snow angel's magic.
The end of the drive.
Snow so sweet, the taste so alive.

Silver sickle,
It screams, "Take me out!"

My pocket is damp,
Silver sickle decided to melt.

Blue wool mittens,
Woven from the touch of age.
I wipe the frost that has built up from a leak in the window,
Silver sickles confine me, stuck on the same page.

These blue mittens hugged the hands of someone I loved,
Who isn't living anymore.

The Struggle Within

I slump in the heart of my beliefs, nowhere near reality,
Clawing away with bitten fingernails at the omnipotent incubi
Tearing pieces of my skin off like children who are curious of
What lies underneath the bark of a tree.

The climax is so close.
I know
The morose angel from the bottomless pit
Will place a note in my lunch box, today,
Praising his best wishes, that I don't make it.

As I wipe away the sweat from above my brows,
Slide my helmet over my head,
And unsheathe my sword from its hilt,
I peer into reality to observe myself before battle.

Like looking through a mirror,
I see myself lying on the kitchen floor.
My head affixed to the rosewood, hands rubbing away
The translucent bricks that skate down my face,
That crash into a superfluity of grief.

I have someone to fight on behalf of,
I have to save myself.

When all of Hell brandishes their wicked Zweihänders, malevolent flails,
Their ballistas staffed by grinning skeletons,
With half a wit of what they are doing,
Shooting recklessly at anything they can,
Hell's grotesque, ash, jagged-toothed gargoyles
Scream and claw at the hot melting rock walls
They have been a part of for too long,
Stalagmites piercing up from the dirt, spearing through shackled slaves,
Empty eye sockets,
And their lead, heavy mallets of splinters thwacking eternally,
Lifting them high above their heads.
Smashing nearby rocks into crumbles,
But the rocks only piece themselves back together seconds later
As if they were never hammered.

The innocent prodded in their backs by dark fallen knights,
With charred onyx armor, and halberds the color of coal,
Into pits of bubbling molten lava,

The world's most evil men ever to exist sit at a heavy, blood- oak table,
Drinking an oozy, grey concoction in human, scrimshaw teacups,
Coughing violently,
But smiling,
As their dictator breaks in through smoldering doors.
Demonites spread their fiery wings and bow,
Embers fall to the ground with each flutter,
To show their honor, they beat the slaves with small, spiked clubs.
The devil chortles to himself as he takes the tea pot and pours himself

Escaped Energy

A cup of grey ooze, He then sees me and stops,
To offer some tea.

I share a cup, the liquid is thick and sweeter than honey,
When the liquid floods my stomach,
The devil and his cohorts disappear and I tread the outskirts of my mind.
It is a time when I was very young,
The lights are serene.
The house is still.

The refrigerator hum echoes, like the comfort of a box fan.
My room is dry, so I pull up the shades and open my window.
Mother and father are roaring at each other on the porch steps.

Cigarette smoke fills the air, and I cough.

Silence.

I quickly jump into bed, and pull the covers over my eyes.
The fighting continues,

I listen even though I know I shouldn't.

I don't like what I hear so I run to my window,
Open my mouth as wide as it can,
And shout.

Shut up!

The commotion freezes, the night's traffic halts for a moment.

A car door slams shut.
His blue shitter drives away. My mother sobs to the wind,
And I feel so goddamn cold.

The night scene fades, I close my eyes.
And when I open them, I have returned from my odyssey.

Barely escaping these maddening worlds,
I pull myself off of the kitchen floor,
Dust my jeans,
Wipe the tears from my eyes,

And consider myself a warrior for standing up to a fear
Meant to pin me down for good.

Though obscurity is everywhere,
We are the absolvers of it, and it is my duty to love myself,
And help anyone who finds themselves on that floor,
Fighting for their life.
You are not alone.

109th Avenue

Malaise. My darkest of gloamings,
Cigarette by the window, eye-rubbed into frustration.   (A saxophone bleeds
The sun hardly rises, behind a tempestuous cloud cover.   through the silence)
There is no comfort,
Albeit, like saltwater to thirst, parodies of paradise,
Difficulties broaden; even complex theories do not imagine solutions.
Such boggling thought,
Prostrated on the floor, chain-smoking cigarettes.
While my forehead is flattened against the glass.

I could lean on these chromatic, celestial walls.
In an endless queue with   (A trumpet wails
Others, frazzled in their own scrutinizing tests,   into the heavens)
Struggling for reason-
Or maybe they have fallen asleep standing.
So I'll crisscross and cut between them all,
To reach the end, because I am certainly not tired,
Where a mirror taller than sky scrapers   (The blue notes blend
Beckons my projected image to come closer.   with heartbeat)

But reflection could not agree with its maker's image,
The other's snapped from their dreams
To pry my eyes away.
Trust within I learned to understand.

Jasper Quince

And beyond me, ignites the sun   (An orchestra strikes in marcato
Dissolving remnants of scattered grey skies,   horns, trumpets, and tubas)
Into the brightest thing my eyes ever saw-

So I follow it
Until my skin tears, splits, and rips off my cheeks & chest.   (Saxophone rumbles
Muscles, tendons, shrivel and snap,   the last word and fades)
My lips dry to dust.
But lucky me. I made it.

❦

I Believe Not Everyone Could Understand

What causes a human break down until their
Thin and brittle bones fracture from the weight of the world?

Starvation is a disciplinary, the drive that forces a tiger
To sink teeth into fur & flesh.   *Glass Eyes*
Many nights, under moons and close shades to it,
The inner peace ruptures-
Starvation awakens an internal drive in me,
But its pain is a grey fierce.
To stand on my own legs can be the most difficult task.
An empty- fueled mind spitting through a grinder,
And poured into a cup of coffee that I drink in replacement of hunger.
But the pain intensifies through blocking thoughts.
I seek an answer.

Once upon a time, I went without food for three days.
On the third night, a man came to my door
And gave me a loaf of bread he had baked, himself.
Why it happened, I will never know,

But why it happened is how I mastered starvation,
My disciplinary.

Sometimes, when caught in the moment,
I admit, that I can lose my kind smile. *Glass Eyes*

Stuck in Time

Tuck your tail between your legs and sit down for a while.
Close your eyes, fold your knees to your chest, and let the walls grow for miles.
Rock bottom, it's the damn darkest place,
Years go by, you let things go, when you can't see your own face;
A vagabond just existing in the exile.

Day by day you watch soil travel through sifters,
Searching for silver and gold,
There are stories that go untold,
By low profile dodgers and one hit drifters,
But they promise everything they needed, was found here, and is now theirs.

You burn twigs in an ever dying fire, turning stones in your palm.
Filling your flask overfull, after the sun goes down.
You think moaning the same old psalms,
About finding value eventually will work, reaching out for petty alms,
But you're unlucky, and will discover poison.

Pedal backwards on black wheels,
Ask yourself how going into something you can't see feels,
And how if you can't pedal on, because you've reached the end,
you might as well get off the bike and walk backwards instead.

Jasper Quince

It's a black hole of a life, and you're in the apex,

No one can touch you, see you exist, feel your pain.

So you keep on writing and getting lost amongst the remains,

Of all your errors and things you need to fix.

There Is Only One Outcome Out of the Legend of the Future

Within our Dark Blue Marble,
Time is domesticated by the force of gravity,

We expect someday, possibly any day,
The sun will crack like an over-boiled egg,
Spewing out lemon, orange, and crimson waves of magma
That gush across a lawless space,
On a path of obliteration,
Slogging on to scorch holes through the Earth
Like automatic bullets rifling through the chest of a mother.

We're blessed to be alive, but humbled to die,
We expect a day of great transition; a divine singularity,
But maybe we should just live in the now,
Where we will always be.

Grey, Gelatinous Whatever

In the hard act of eyes, I've judged with momentum.
A sweeping weakness of mine
That leaves an innocent soul to wander the desert of desire,
Digging up sparkles that disintegrate.
To learn that the only thing that can replace fear is
Your permission for it to pass through you.
A danger, and everyone's a victim.
How I swear, and how I close my eyes,
To watch the sun rise, in pallets of orange, red, and tan.
Even as wise as I think I am, I'm astounded by how little
I understand.
Springing from a coil of disbelief,
To raise my hopes like waves on a full moon,
Is a rare cosmic occurrence.
History of its past resembles the beheaded chicken on the block,
Dumb bastard…
The full moon elicits blood from the savage.
And a hunger for prey that seems so small in the act of your eyes,
That your judgments could harm a fly.
Shoo.

In My 6th Grade Shoes

Neatly tucked in my back pocket,
A mysterious note,
A perplexing pipe system,
Folded so many times,
I wonder if it was ever truly meant to be opened.

The scent of a woman,
Or the desire to become one,
A perfume so pungent,
It screams to be opened.
But I don't think I will.

Hearts,
Dance around the letters that create my name,
Penciled in shades of timber wolf and smoke.
The world's most beautiful play,
And some people are crying.
But I'm not.

Given from a friend, of a friend,
Of a friend....
So the story tells,

Jasper Quince

And I am
Perplexed and sallow in study hall,
Fingers clenched around the note,
Fright against the nature of curious love.

My teacher pulls me aside after class,
Discerning my peculiar behaviors,
Witnessing me
Slide under my seat,
To catch a glimpse of the note,
During our reading skills quiz.

My face boils scarlet,
Skin tingles,
I let her in on my secret
She lightly smiles
Understanding these mature emotions,
And folds my hand with hers,
Over the note.
Read it.

But I will not read it.
But I cannot escape it.
And I will not,
And I will at the same time.
Throw it away, tear it up into polygenic scraps,
And blow away the torment.

At lunch the children wiggle at their tables,
Anxious for recess to begin.

Escaped Energy

I sit lackluster, chewing my cud.
Skin like raw chicken,
Fingers tracing the edge of the note,
Handled so many times, the edges are frittering
Into dust.

I hold the note up to the light, in dire hopes of cheating,
But all I see is black.

After the day is finished,
I find a vacant seat on the bus.
Open the window to breath in the fresh air.
I sit in the back seat,
And crouch down to where the dirty shoes, dust clumps,
And gum wads collect.

After everyone finds their own special spot on the bus,
I slide the knife-like note from my sheath.
Same as it had been all along,
Penciled in, now smudging, from wear and tear.

My fingers dig between the folds, and pull like untethering the roasted bird.
Flaps are out, their points so sharp, pointing at me, pointing at my heart,
My face.
Until in front of me, is a single sheet of paper, no two,
Pressed firmly against each other, never wanting to part.
The ink sticks just a tad to the pages.
I rip them apart.
And dare to read.

⁓⟐⁓

Song of Repose

Waltzing with a white rose,
Freshly picked and de-thorned,
Twirling like a fallen leaf in September,
My eyes lacquered in a vicarious dream.

A peddler on the boardwalk,

Where the ocean continuously breathes,
Pours out a sonata that
Tames the waves.

And when I am in his presence,
He sits, legs crossed, and stares through me;
An aged, acoustic guitar wedged in between
His rugged lap and his frail chest.

I reach in my back pocket for my wallet.
-Save your pity for someone else.
Disheveled, discolored beard,
Teeth coated in decades of nicotine,
Hands hold a tremble,
Eyes dark as a widow.

Escaped Energy

The peddler begins to play again.
His left foot bobbing to the beat,
Fingers dancing up and down the fret board
With an uncanny agility.

He turns his face to the sky,
And expels a grizzly voice from deep within his lungs.
I sit down cross-legged,
Close my eyes,

And nine minutes escape my clutches.

When the melodies end,

He lays his guitar on the ground,
Still humming, And says,
-It's not for the money.

The peddler pulls himself off the ground,
And picks up his instrument.
Leaving me behind with an ocean breeze,
The boardwalk,
And the sting of simplicity,
My thoughts still musing on what just occurred,

❧

The Moon Over the Mountain

It was an August summery swelter,
But Violet Roves was determined
To climb a verdant, broccoli-bundled mountain,
To catch a recherché, Sturgeon Supermoon
That would emerge from the rounded peak hours before dusk.
This day celebrated her ninth wedding anniversary;
She had promised the moon for her husband, her soul mate,
Who shared an avidity for the mysteries of space and everything beyond.

The sun began its descent into a dipping valley opposite the mountain,
Still, there was enough vigor to guide Violet's long,
Pencil legs up the rotund base like a threading needle.
The further she ascended, the evergreens agglomerated.
Sunrays could not protrude through the medley of robust leaves
Which maintained a coolness that was calming.

After puzzling in circles for an hour,
Violet felt completely lost inside the belly of the intricate, deceitful forest.
The compass in her mind gyrated in a frenzy.
Her calendula eyes raced between the trunks,
But every way bore a resemblance to the other.

She surrendered,
Supine, in the years of dead leaves,
And studied the gaps between the branches
That tried to hide a darkening cyan sky.
She thought about her husband,
His bold, brown eyes, thick, auburn hair, granite smile,
Worrying why Violet was so late coming home.

The sky toasted and transitioned to a starlight escape,
Violet still in contemplation,
Listened to the owls call out, the wolves bellow into the eve-
The echoes of crunching twigs and leaves,
Snapping her trailing thoughts of blue serenity.
Fire from afar grasped her attention,
A lantern in the distance swung like a pendulum,
Hypnotizing her eyes.

Violet squeezed out a shout through her pulsating windpipe,
"Is there anybody out there?"
But there was no response; she fervently wandered toward the light,
Brushing the leaves out of her dangling, umber locks.

Beheld,
A frail, four-foot tall, human-esque creature behind a mask of twisted bone
That spiraled up and flattened above its head like antennae.
Carved into the bone plate were two tiny slits
For two beady dots the fire reflected upon.
The mask lacked a mouth hole,
And pointedly extended to the creature's collarbone,

It stood like stone in a deerskin-strapped jumpsuit,
In one hand, grasping a majestic, ironwood rod,
The other, a crosshatched, wire lantern with a tiny white candle inside
That seemed to light more around than it should.

The wooded creature bowed in her presence, then looked up to the sky,
The pause was wrenching, until Violet broke the silence,
"Who are you?"
The mask gradually lowered back down and the creature closely speculated
Violet.
It swung its lantern forward, for her to follow,
And she complied without question.
She gazed up to the moon, impossibly higher than ever,
But unusually larger in retrospect.

Passing bulged formations of rock, and fallen pines,
They slithered & stepped over obstacles scattered in the woods
Until the air was thin.

A lazy floating fog around the vicinage gracefully formulated
In front of the maestro with the lantern into a spiral stairway.
Without looking back, it climbed up, up, up, above the mountain,
Where only daring birds could soar.
"Wait for me!"
Violet planted a foot on the first cloud step, but it fell through.
She looked up, perplexed, seeking an answer, but the lantern had vanished,
The clouds in front of her dissolved in a sudden gust of whirling wind.

Like drawn back drapes to a window, she was given sight to her surroundings.
The woodland creature had led her to the summit of the mountain,
Every star, the milk spilled galaxy, the blackness in between was vivid,
And the moon was up close.

But now Violet was more lost than ever on top the mountain,
Still without the moon for her husband, and no route to make it home.
She sat on a mound of thin grass, throwing her face in her palms,
And began to cry at her hapless fortune and doltish ideas.
Tonight, Violet had abused their anniversary beyond reasoning,
She pictured her husband somberly pouring glass after glass of Red Cabernet,
Drinking himself drunk out of shame,
Staring out the window with melted eyes.
She wept below the moon, on top the world.
"I should have known better…"

A string of heated tears trickled to fall under the strict laws of gravity-
But, this time, they fell up. Three special, sparkling droplets rose to her eyes
And fluttered into the night like bats of diamond,
Migrating towards the moon.

She swiftly rose, and watched the tears fly beyond her sight,
Then disappearing amongst the twinkling lights. She hopelessly sighed.
"Now I must have gone insane."
After an anxious minute, she kicked at a loose pebble.

The moon in full jiggled from its place.
Then it shook left to right, right to left,

Violet fell back in shock back on the grassy mound.
An invisible weight pinned her down, as if the blades of grass
Had bloomed into thorny vines, and wrapped their barbs into her skin.
"Help, somebody!"
The moon vehemently quaked,
She flailed her head around, trying to free her body.
Then it dropped.

Violet cut into a bewildered scream,
The Earth under her feet spun a little faster.
The moon quickly grew larger and larger,
Its pocked smile turned into a monster with intricate, jagged fangs,
Readied to devour her and everyone.

The moon's mass replaced the sky.
The mountain serenaded in an intense luminescent, glow.
She searched around for hope. An escape. A cave between two rocks.
The weight from her suddenly lifted. She sprung up on her pencil legs,
And ran for her life, transgressing from unknowing abyss,
To nothingness,
Sight dividing white to black.
Violet blindly rushed as far as she could until-

The world quavered, as if jabbed in the temple for the knockout;
The moon had struck the mountain.
A deafening boom stole sound, everything jerked to a rigid halt,
Violet's body was thrown against a wall, white light surged into the cave.
She felt the blood rampantly spill from her head and fingers.

The next five minutes were a continuous roar of rock punching rock,
Sad groans from the Earth, the ground underneath
Diverged into fissures, swallowing fallen debris from the ceiling.
She lied on her side, cheek on the floor, stiff with fear.

Nothing mattered when the world was ending
And dreams from the sky dropped and died like birds.
Violet embraced the Earth and prepared
To be expunged from that of what she destroyed.
That white light seeping into the entrance
Cracked and divided by the longsword of darkness.
The moon wall released a high-pitched piercing, din.
Spider-webbing cracks crawled up from the bottom.
Then it disintegrated, splintered, crumbling away into a billion snowflakes.
Everything flicked to a hollow black and all was silent, except the echo of
Ringing.

Violet heaved and coughed, struggling to intake dust laced oxygen,
Though sightless, her other senses were miraculously functional.
She smelled the soil packed up her nose, tasted the fresh blood on her lips,
Stroked loose grit beneath her fingers, and heard a soft sobbing behind her.
Violet reluctantly pulled her sore body to a knee from the floor
And peered back.
Deeper in the cave a fire light coruscated along the walls.
She stumbled towards it.

In a corner, a lantern with a tiny white candle
Flickered silhouettes on stone.
The Woodland creature lied facedown, beside it, unmoving.

Its mask by its side, broken like a Christmas ornament.
The creature bled from its purplish, venous forehead, coating its entire face,
Collected in a divot of its shallow, concave cheek,
And dribbled to a splotch next to the lamp.

One hand was clenched around its wooden staff,
But the other hand had a finger that pointed
Back towards the entrance of the cave.
There was no room for words, through all the thoughts, at a time like this.
Violet, turned around, holding onto the wall for support,
And she hobbled out of the cave.

She looked to the sky for answers. The moon was nowhere in sight.
"My god, the world has lost its most valuable jewel, all because of me."
Violet Roves bowed her head,
Kenning she might be the only person left on Earth.

She whispered to the wind that prodded her misery.
"What is this, and what is loneliness?
Where is life when what you ask for is too much?
And if sometimes you get what you ask for,
At what cost does it affect the remaining without?"

The ground was soft, but crunchy beneath her feet.
Moon dust and preserved shards coated the mountain grey.
Everywhere, trees lay like fallen men,
Impacted in the ground, sticks reaching out for help through the cosmic snow.
The mountain had risen higher,
And the valley below looked like a wrinkle on skin.

Escaped Energy

Violet contemplated retreating to the cave again, but the light douses,
A pained sigh carried along the curls of a gusty wind.
There was nothing left- but to scale the mountain down.

Violet ruminated on where the lone survivor,
Who snuffed mankind, went to find peace.
She pursed her lips to the worst thoughts in the cavities of her head,
Searched for the worst way to follow through with them
And discovered something worse than that.

The cloud spiral stairway formed once again in front of her.
This time, when she put a foot on the first step, it concretely held.
Violet climbed up, up, up, in hope there was something at the top
To replace her rotted heart.

The stairs tightly coiled making Violet so dizzy
The stars seemed to huddle around her limp soul.

Eventually she reached the apex, there was no floor or next step.
She tried to see if there was any sign of life below,
But all around, the world was a barren bowl of dirt, toothpicks, and dark rock.
She pointed her nose to the sky,
Brushed her hair back behind an ear, and cried out,
"I'm so sorry. I can't go on like this, knowing I have destroyed everything
Because I wanted something I wasn't supposed to have.
I didn't know it would end this way.
Never forgive me."

She let herself free, and dropped. Falling! Falling… falling-
The stars became strands of light, like comets with long tails.
Thoughts in her head mashed together into what was and what would
Never be,
But it was a peace she could die with- even infinity had to end eventually.

The strands united in swirls of color
And painted her husband's glinting facial qualities.
His spectacular aura comforted her with affirmation,
Everything's okay,
Held her fingers and pressed them to his lips…

When Violet was a toddler, she used to sneak out the window
And walk along the roof of her house.
One night, staring at the moon, she pushed a spoon through the night sky
with one eye open, tried to scoop up the moon, and gobble it up.
But she had lost her footing and toppled off the roof.
She should have died,
But the next thing she remembered was her father,
Her sitting on his broad shoulders, as he called out,
Where's the moon?

Now, Violet was swooped up by something too large,
A lustrous, incandescent, white gondola that swam through the sea of night,
Speeding faster than she was falling.
It glided twice around the peak of the mountain and then slingshot away.
Violet reached her fingertips out to the mountain as if to grab a hold of it,
Attempting to anchor the white ship to dock.

Then she snapped from the shock of death, rolled on her stomach,
And suctioned her body to stone –
Why, it was the moon.
All had not been destroyed.
Violet was flooded with hope, jollified at what she saw.
She stood on her feet
And walked forward to the crescent's prow.
Her open wounds had seamed and healed, blood, cleansed from her face.
The wind blew her hair back, wildly whipping like excited tails,
Her eyes were spirited, again, flashing sunbursts.
The moon was not down.

In fact, the moon was very much alive-
It brought Violet around the world in a hurried blur.
Then it descended into an ocean, as a boat,
Creating tsunamis that spread like expanding ringlets.

In midst of the mesmerizing moment,
Something from behind Violet tapped her shoulder.
She turned to find it was woodland creature unmasked,
Grinning with ice-clear teeth that diffracted from moonlight,
Hopping up and down in excitement.
Its face was healed of all wounds.
She smiled back, and everything felt right.

The creature opened a knapsack and pulled out a newly constructed mask
Carved out of the same material as the moon,
In similar fashion to the old one of bone.
It then smashed off one of the ears. The piece snapped like a wishbone.

The creature picked the piece up and held it out to Violet.
She let the creature place the selenite spike of moon in her hands.

The warm smoothness of cratered rock
Removed the feeling of sorrow from her face, her eyes, her mind.
The creature in the mask waved its stick in the air.
Glimmering dust spread from the knotted end.
Then it slipped on its uneven mask.

The moon sailed on, cutting through the vast open ocean.
The creature took Violet by her fingers
And brought her to the very edge of the moon's pointed prow.
She held the moonstone ear to her chest and looked up to the stars,
Beaming over finally obtaining the moon for her husband.

Suddenly, the creature in the mask dropped its stick
And quickly pushed Violet off the moon into the dark, foreboding waters.
The ocean swallowed her body, covering her mouth with cold liquid hands.
She sank beneath the waves, watching the crescent sail on without her.
Violet struggled to regain composure, but she sank like a bag of stones,
Further, and further, the white light dimmed, a whisper, then pinched out.
She hit rock bottom, and once again, there was nothing.

Violet's hope had been compromised again,
She felt, out of everything that she had endured,
Truly there was no way to escape this time.
She opened her eyes- still holding her breath.
A lantern's light shined inside a cave in front of her.

She swam with one hand, the other
Holding onto the moon shard, kicking with her legs.
Her lungs squeezed the remaining oxygen from her body, begging to inhale.
The light grew, the closer she got, but underwater, everything was fuzzy.
Violet pleaded her body to hold from
Breathing in the heavy water just a little longer.
She would not let go of the world. She had come too far to end here.
With a final push, she broke the darkness, her lungs gave way, to pull.

Pull air. Sweet silver air.
Violet Roves had not drowned. She gasped and absorbed in that silver air,
Sprawled on the rocky ground and laid there until she had had her fill.
She stood on wobbly legs and noticed from the opposite way,
There was a pale white light.
Violet held onto the wall and followed it,
Knowing through this whole ordeal she had been through,
To trust that white light no matter what.

The light pulled her out of the hole.
There, hanging in the night sky, floating with the heavens,
The Sturgeon Supermoon.
She hopped up and down, ecstatic to be alive,
To not have broken the world she loved so much.
The moon was over the mountain, once again.

Uncannily, the moonstone still rested in her palm,
The rock she suffered so much to obtain.
A great piece of raw stone, presenting itself
Warmer than the touch of another's hand.

Once again, she was lost between the trees at the top of the mountain.
Holding the rock, though, she felt capable of guiding herself down.
After an hour she had made it to the base again.

The sky blended from a lavish deep blue,
To an amethyst purple when Violet made it to the bottom, still soaked,
Still holding the moonstone, still alive.

She couldn't wait to bring it home to her husband.

Things That Matter

So inexplicably,
The sun explodes the dark night
To an obliteration of taught, smelting piano-wires,
Sharp and keen.

My eyes grow wide as the sky of our Mother Earth shouts out to the roosters,
The clocks,
The moon. *Your reign is over for now.*

How set in stone these natural wonders
Occur & presume like a replaying movie.
Something supreme glitters the dewy grass, the hard sand,
The eyes of the children bumbling to class.

It's the natural beauty we all assume,
But I relish in it every day.
I let it seize me by the throat,
Squeeze the air from my lungs,
And tingle through my bloodstream.

Imagine if the sun was a spotty, disperser of light droplets.
And we would harvest it by the bucket, filling pails full.
I'd guzzle a gallon a day.

I love the Georgia peach sunrise, as I romance the Brooklyn
Pale sunset.
After long days, where the mind has fallen miles
Behind the body, it is easy to walk into
Walls or place the sugar in the refrigerator.
But I want more.
I'd like to
Force the young and old, terrorists to Americans,
Politicians to politicians,
That the sun only rises once a day,
Isn't that wrong to take for granted?

No Title: v

Somewhere,
High above vicinity of casual eyesight,
A supermarket blares Lady Gaga,
While carts push themselves,
And listeners load in heedless rhythm.

Somewhere,
The Laundromat plays a dreamscape disco
That mollifies moods,
And propels tedious activities, such as folding clothes,
With bursts of nirvana.

Downtown Salem, Mass,
Late, on a Thursday night,
The bars are playing music too.
And it brings me to the thought…

Music can elicit feelings I cannot begin to describe.
I can only illustrate its symptoms.

Gooseflesh that spreads up the arms,
Head teetering, eyes that gently close,
Elations so superlative,
That when the song ends, I could too.

Minds that tingle, death could come at any moment,
And it'd catch me with the greatest grin I've ever produced.

Music that causes your emotions to flow like rapid rivers,
Passionate in their nature to exalt salt from the sea.

I once drove home after grim news I wouldn't graduate high school.
The stereo screaming,
Instability,
A feeling of nothingness,
Like the outer edges of space. Music saved me, though.

Romanced ampflication; Song.
A dual rhythm of bodies in motion,
Flushed cheeks,
And ardent passions that twist and burst asunder.

Many a time, music evokes tears from my eyes,
If my ears could cry, they would too.

We relate to one another through genre.
Rap, the sharp and catchy poetry of the modern culture.
Country, where the sun goes down,
And pungent lyrics about mourning lost love, or life.

The punk scene, passion in something
That isn't religion, government, or media.
Classic rock, the temperament of guitars,
Played like extra limbs.

Escaped Energy

Most artists claim music is a lending hand to create.

Why do we love music so much,
To flail our arms in the air,
Or nods our heads
Or tap our toes…

I don't know.

I just love to feel.

1994, the Stars, and
My Plastic Spoon

Tonight is my bowl of cereal.
Back from trick - or - treating,
I pull back my Power Rangers mask

And lay in costume on the hood of my aunt's
Cerulean 91' wood-paneled station wagon,
Guiding a cracked, plastic spoon across the galaxy,
Pushing it through the soupy nothingness like a space shuttle.

Alas, Discovery.

I close one eye,

Scoop the shiny loot into my spade,

Bring them to my curious lips,
Chew them into mush,

And swallow with a glass of Milky Way on the side.

Escaped Energy

The ivory moon glares at me
As if I plucked its children from their cribs.

My heart weakens and I regret my silly intentions.
I fling the disposable weapon to the ground.

I'm sorry Ms. Moon.

I open my mouth,
Reach with my tiny fingers
Deep into my black hole and pull out, like popcorn on a string,
The little dipper, Orion's belt,
And the North Star.
I fling them back into the sky and they soar up with tails of fire.

The constellations gently drift back to their beds.
I slide off the car, and bend over to pick up my pillowcase of candy.
I can't wait to go home and look at my work through the telescope.

A Bed's Tale

He's on his back in bed, looking through the ceiling, remembering a night sky.
Has a thought nailed in place, he hammered it himself,
It's firm in the third eye.
He thinks upon the hour, holds the hands of clocks, to slow down time.
Eventually, he lets go, as the sun does, too,
Now he sees obscure clouds that block all remnants of light.

A half eaten slab of chocolate cake, a worn book hardly read,
He cannot finish either, silently in thought instead.
He thinks so much his eyes burn and crack red,
Tigers, tearing him limb-by-limb, thread-by-thread.

He thinks about his past, what it was like to be a kid again,
He can see his little hands causing trouble where he had forgotten.
Reaching into a fish tank and ripping out the fish,
Tossing them on the floor, watching them gasp for oxygen.

He thinks about the present, and it makes him squirm beneath his blanket.
He can only see around him, his every-things taped away in boxes.
A home that isn't his,
He is an exhibit, in a house, he is a trinket.

He thinks about the future, riding atop a black cloud,
Pages of his writing, swallowed in the shroud,

He reaches inside to pull them out,
And when he grabs a hold, he pulls a plug, and falls on his ass to the ground.

Today, to tonight, to dawn, not even classical music can make him sound,
So he pretends to dream like he has accomplished a lot,
He makes it to the sun, by hopping stars,
And puts on his solar reflective shoes,
And walks the whole thing round.

Wintertime Shock

We trek to the post office through A-bombs of snow squalls.
Our cold, watery lives perch atop my mother's head,
Melting through her copper hair, and into her thick skull,
Delivering a reactionary brain freeze.

Incongruously,
Mother will tear your heart out like a blade of grass,
In the hands of some summer girl dancing in the fields;
An ensemble of war trumpets flapping out of key behind the clouds.

I don't have much to say about my-small-self, except
My name is Atlas and I act older than I should.

Shreds of soaked and scattering newspaper
Toss against fences that follow the sidewalk,
Like rustled feathers in a chicken coop.
Our right bears an abandoned county jail,
Cement walls sky high.

But today, between the iron gates
And beyond them iron doors,
And within those iron windows,
A light burns within, someone is inside.
Mad- minded Mother hurries past without noticing.

Escaped Energy

Snow rises past my knees.
A plow truck bursts through the veil of blizzad with a thunderous grumble,
Scraping metal against pavement.
I clench mother's hand in mine, but am lost
In a moment of awe-
A blinking shark of the great white sno'cean,
Stuffing its steel jaws with frigid, flesh.
Leaving its trail through salt chunks & sand.
It passes, or we pass it,
The lights slowly fade to white.
And the grumble quiets.
My hustle is reduced to a waddle.

Mother grabs my hand, and forces my small legs to churn faster.
Ahead, an undisturbed mass of sparkling snow,
Frosting on the birthday cake.
I clip and drag a thin layer off the top with each step;
I want to turn around so badly.

I watch Mother's jeans with cautious eyes
As globs of slush squirt from the tips of my boots,
Surely, soaking those pants through.
But she does not know
Or doesn't care.

My arm aches from the tugging game between mother and I.
The post office is close enough,
But I am an anchor on this speedboat.
Pickup is a necessity.

But, then our hands rip apart,
I lose my reigns.
Skidding boots and snow impacted gloves, I spinout in the snow,
While Mother's shape tapers into that white curtain.

I spit out a shark's amount of snow,
Dribbling its way down my chin and slipping into my jacket.

I am young and it sears my skin and I cry.
The anchor is snagged and lost its chain
The sharks are going to eat me-

But these rare times, when the worst has won,
Even it has its limits.
A great arm clasps around my body and lifts me to the clouds and grey skies.
Fore it is Mother! I flip up like a caught fish,
Land on two boots, and slap myself snow free-
"Come on you little brat!" She sneers.

Mourning Blues

Dip my Nikes in a city,
Where they click to beats under flickering street lamps.
I'm pointing at windows with pretty every-things
But what makes it perfect is-
I'm in the city with you.

I'm growing up and getting ready.
Adventure here I am- but I don't know much from there.
I bore from dried days, mourning blues, lost working until I bear wrinkles,
Slipping gears of concentration; what to be and where.
I want to remember each melody like a hit single.
Blue skies, brown eyes, not sure why,
The path seems appropriate with you.

I'm bursting wings from my fingers,
And I want to fly my writing on thru,
To gently make you feel special,
So our struggle isn't so long.
I'm not fortunate to be an angel but,
We'll get somewhere someday,
Creating a saccharine halo around our heads.

Life is about the strangest surprises.

Where, you think you know one thing,

And that one thing is more than just one thing,

It is a lot of things,

Then it is a book's length and you haven't a clue where to begin.

But the answer is at the end.

And I know you hate page skipping,

So read on. I think we're getting to the good part.

A Willow's Kiss
(Yellow Boat Part ii)

Here's to another midnight,
Carrying the weight of a dragnet,
Full of dead newts and snapped cattails,
Deep along the dark layers of the ocean of my emotions.
My eyes strain to see the glint of light of which I came from,
As it shrinks to a pin hole,
I am not sure if I ever existed.

Sometimes, the fear of loneliness, has no control,

Moments in life provide new hope, as well as take away pacifiers; lessons.
Legs were made for the restless that cannot sleep,

And so I utilize them, leaving the nest that is a distraction.

The cold air is violent, but I relate with its abuse.
The stars are absent,
But the cities lights guide my thoughts down the path,
Until I break from reality and walk upon a new trail.

The moon curiously peers out,

Jasper Quince

And for a brief moment,

Everything is illuminated in a pale white glow.
The ground is moist.
The ocean ripples neatly in the distance.
The wind shatters the peace,
and a sudden shiver

Makes the joints in my arms and legs ache.

At the bend of the trail,
A
Wooden bench for one
Invites me to sit and rest,
So I comply.

I close my eyes, and let the air do the talking.
The wind whips wildly, drowning sound like a waterfall.
My throat expels the pent up emotions held inside.
The bench listens intently, never interrupting.
After I share a piece of myself with the bench,

I humbly pat the seat,

And the bench shares a piece of itself with me.

My index finger throbs with a fresh splinter,

Escaped Energy

But I am not upset.

This was the only way the bench could show me that

It understood.
I rise to resist the power of gravity, always trying to hold us down.

Continuing to walk slowly down the black path,
I come across the dark outlines of a flock of geese
Squawking at the pearl in the sky playing peek-a-boo,
Piercing through the wind's clamor.
My body is frozen like the edges of the water,
As they gracefully fall into line;
Less worries than I will ever have in my life.

After a brief pause of nature's little miracles,
My journey continues.
My searching for SOMETHING,

Finds me another bench.

But this one is positioned next to a willow,

A sage of the wood, with multitudes of leafy tendrils,

The wind passionately blows its drooping branches around,

And I get the feeling this tree has a beating heart within.

Jasper Quince

I step closer.
Its shriveled fingers brush against my face.
The tree is lonely and needs to touch, affection,
To see me for who I am.

I clamp my fingers around the outstretched leafy fingers,

And pull them up against my face.

The rough scraping, releases my emotions,
This time in the form of warm tears down my cheeks.

I received a message from the tree,

Everything is okay, has been okay, and will always be okay.

I shared a bond with two inanimate objects tonight,
I leave the bench and the gentle willow,
And take the path guided by city lights
Back to my home,
Feeling less alone, knowing though I am in pain, it's okay.
Natural as being alive,
This world is the most beautiful place to be in the universe.

Warming to Change (Yellow Boat Part iii)

Goodbye, Yellow Boat. I
Untied your leash from the dock,
The willow wept.
And I never looked back,
The gentle hand-like waves took you away.

Cradled inside, wrapped within a tarp,
Was everything that I learned to let go.
Lucky numbered letters, materialistic gifts, aching pictures,
We were the wild things, but only for a minute.
Cans of spray paint and the idea being cool.
Goodbye, old love.
Life is more than just this small sanctuary,
I live to love the Earth, and long to discover more and more loves.
Saying goodbye is the hardest part,
But all that stays is my gold and grey reality.

Felix!

Ship away,
Shift like the waves,
Roll through the thunder,
Pray against the graves.
Felix! Felix.
Hold your tattered sails,
Escape the sharks and whales,
The captain is enraged,
Listen to his woes and wails,
A sordid fairy tale.
FELIX!
A sinking feeling never lies,
It's wrong to tell a boy that men don't cry.
Felix!
Surely everyone will die.
Felix!
The gully knife- cutting wind blows a mighty blast,
And while the yellow boat collects water,
I can only think, "Felix!"
Wrapped in a past.
"Help!" The passengers squeal.
"Felix," I cry.

I Am...

I am cunning as a fox,

Swift as a threatened weasel.
My intelligence is sharp like a hawk's eyesight,
While my eyesight is as keen as an eagle.

I'm the elephant forgetter,
Chameleon personality changer.
I am the delectable apple from the ripe apple tree.

I am the bee's wings that fly you where you need to be.
I am the snide of the snake,
And the whale's appetite.
I am the cat's purr,
But the lion's might.

I carry eight times my weight,
Like a fire ant, and when I'm upset,
I can bench a hundred times that.

I carry the friskiness of a Halfmoon Betta fish,
My dignified wisdom won't find me on any sailor's dish.

Jasper Quince

The boldness of a Great White appears when I puff out my chest,
I am a Kodiak bear when you spot me catching some rest.

I am solely the things I wish me to be,
I am my imagination, and I am my reality.

I am more than you could ever see.

Joko Lenno

Beneath the sunlight,
Dividing thick fogs,
Two people-in-love
Sway left to   Right, to
Left to   Right, to...
As they promenade
Through an ocean of sticky leaves,
Freshly pressed and covered
In a glistening slick of rain.

Life is temporary.
Death remains forever;
Unchanging.

The fog fritters into the air above,
Revealing Maples, Oaks, and sparse Birches
That have given a part of themselves,
To feel the rhythm of hearts in love.

Death worries not for whom it takes,
It worships quantity.

Jasper Quince

In the upcoming distance,
Erect in a flourishing meadow,
A white house two stories tall,
Welcomes its owners Home.

Death is necessary.
But ends where they should not meet?
I guess that is reality.

He rests his fingers upon the frigid keys from his piano,
(Always playing at sunup)
And begins with an E major chord.
She, waltzes 'round the room,
Raising the blinds to let in the sun,
Opening windows to let in the fresh air,
And when she has finished,

She ensconces herself beside him,
Left leg pressed lightly upon his right.

And he plays on.

Locomotivation to the Sun

My knees are bent, poles in each glove, scraping dust off the top layer of a
Snowy crag, I bowl down on skis,
The wind cracking eggs against my face.
Time built this steep ramp that lies just ahead,
And I am prepared
To fly on past Earth's skies in gold- winged boots,
To catch a locomotive stopping at the thin air of stratosphere,
That makes its destination around our sun,
Where I will have a long time to read my favorite books in between.

And on my way,
Crossing a black carpet of infinite diamond dust,
I'll unlace my golden boots,
And give them to a child in the caboose
That reminds me of myself when I was young,

When I took my first trip.
I cried and begged to go home, clawing at the windows like a frazzled animal.
Then a tall man in a bowler hat handed me his wings,
Make sure you are happy with who you are now,
Because you have the rest of your life to be that person.
And I flew home to Earth with my wings between my legs,
Thanking life for giving me another chance.

Jasper Quince

The kid disappears like the light of a dead star,
But there's more life in that direction than where I am going.
Where I doubt myself again,
Feeling the underneath of my seat with fingertips,
And pushing my forehead against the window.

So I'll stretch my legs across the vacant seat next to me
And fall asleep to the bumps of asteroids pelting the roof.
I don't want to wake until reaching something meaningful.

The Blues

Blues are the crush you can't have.
The juice without the orange,
A summer without sun.
The Blues pull your eyes like blinds,
They tunnel down your throat to the bottom of your tub,
The Blues scrape the edges clean, until you moan and
Ache… But don't you feel better?

The Blues paint Picasso's beauty,
Sing Ray Charles' melodies,
Cause a grown man to cry.
The Blues are the most human thing about us, though.

The Blues tend to hide in speakeasies,
Where the times are tough.
The Blues serve stiff drinks and play gloomy pool,
The Blues stumble out that door each night, one by one.

Alas, The Blues are looking out for one another,
Sparing change to the homeless because it can relate,
Friends who comfort those in break ups.
The Blues know sadness,

Just as the scientists thwarted of their pertinent data on climate change.
If we don't do something now,
The planet will suffer from The Blues.

The Reds

Long beaten tired on the dead of night,
The cusp of something sculpting inside me, unzips my skin,
Unravels knotted tendons, to scratch a rusted nail against my bones.
But I am at peace, through the thick comings that are seemingly bleak.

While the red streetlights hum in Boston,
 I am at rhythm with the soft echo of a slap guitar player
Jumbling out his heart for no one but himself.
I watch the geyser of a fountain,
Push the red reflecting water up, in a fancy parade of sparkle.
Still motion, I want to leap from this bench to ascend to its rosy plateau,
Dancing on water to bring me higher.
But it just falls, and I settle for this moment.

Long beaten tired on the night with death,
The backbones of a spiny saguaro stand proudly.
Bereaved of water for months,
Rots, one upheld arm, while the other has fallen off some time ago.
Like a dartboard, pinholes burrow
Through its torso from birds seeking shade or water,
Though it manages to bloom a pink, dish-sized flower with golden frills
Within.

Jasper Quince

While looking down from 10,000 feet above sea level,

Into a red ocean of brushes, brambles, and ironwood trees,

The howl of an owl reverberates between two orange mountains in Sedona.

I am led to Devil's Cliff and I let my feet dangle into the abyss,

Imagining an orchestra curating my emotions of

A tide twisting frenzy, euphoria,

And peace.

The Potente of Krimson...

Through flowered fields of humble green,
Within a ring of evergreens,
An ancient church crumbled into a stream,
What stands alone, a stone door waits for its key.

A vile whisper slips between the cracks, carried on a fated breeze,
Transforming to a shout when it gets to where it needs.
Someone listens, in his citadel atop a hill,
That looms before its hamlet in the valley.
Open me.

Through The King's bloodshot eyes, cajoled by a coveted prize.
Born to sit on the throne from luxurious demise,
The less sense, the more wise,
The secret key is his ethereal divine,
Dangling from his matriarch's neck it lies.

One frosty night in early spring, the king has his fortuitous dream,
Outside his palace, the vision guides him past the hill,
Along a sparkling stream,
To a water hole, where trout catch flies, and everything's serene.
There, The Queen is picking tulips by the edge for The King.
She senses an added presence, a door appearing from nothing,

It groans and begs, as a child,
Open me, I'm trapped, let me free.
Everything is bathed in white, and difficult to see.
She drifts closer to its call, manipulated by curiosity,
When suddenly The Queen's flesh melts from her body,
Her eyes roll into the water, and her bones carried away with the breeze.
The key opens something sealed away for a century.
And The King drools in dream,
Where the door has done what it and him had agreed.

The Potente of Krimson awakens, blood of the Queen's stains his lap-
He wears a truculent grin as his tearful eyes roll back,
A crow's cackle escapes his lungs, a fitting cough he wracks.
The crimson king took to his seat, the blood ran down his back.

Blood flows from his golden throne and spatters on the marble floor,
The servants near wait for his command,
Though they quiver in their drawers,
He licks his crimson hands, and points a dagger to the door,
And only then did he cry, "Let it rain! Let it pour!
Come back with everything, loot the den until there's nothing more!"
Run, rabbit, redrum.

... And His Crimson Hands

All that beats is dead and gone, the family pets and plants,
Within the forlorn cottages, where time is in suspense.
A humble merchant visits from a village to vouch her credence,
Instead she bows her head and gives her blessings for their lack of presence,
Looking through a murky window that once housed a friend.

The hamlet's men had heard the lore of boundless gold and gems,
One by one, they stomped a path,
To the ominous door where The King had sent them.
Not one came back, so he sent the women,
And then he sacrificed the children.
Blinded by the curse, The King sits alone, the last of his kingdom.

Come one, come all.

The agreement was not complete, and so The King
Grabs his steed to meet what lurked by the stream.
His stomach twisted, mind awry, for the first time he sees clearly,
But it is all too late, the vile voice begins to sing,
To sooth the purity arisen in the heart of The Krimson King.

And when he opens the door, inside is black and cold,
The wind pushes him inside and the doors quickly close,

Beheld his presence, the darkest thing he could have possibly composed,
It was unerringly him, another king on a throne of bones,
Licking fresh blood on his fingers.
I am King Incarnadine.

You are to be locked away for many excruciating centuries.
You are the last key, and now I am the ruler of everything.

And with that, The Potente of Krimson never again was seen.

All that remains is King Incarnadine.

Summer Nights

The jagged and fiery day fizzles.
Cool air brings relief to dry lungs
That pulled in the heat from the summer day,
It's the nights though, that enchant the season.

The evenings ripen.
And the only place I'd want to be is outside.
Calm as a mourning dove in its nest,
Relaxing like the war is over.

It's nights like these that build courage
To dance, love, drink, desire.
The nights make you sweat through passion and effort,
The same ones that make me feel beautiful inside and out.

A New Chapter

Out with the old, turn the page for something new.
I wear a badge of embarkment to let everyone know
I'm prepared and open to new ideas.
Care to cater my entertainment?

Set me straight as the horizon, day and night predictability?
For now, I'll raise hell and cacophony, prevalent but impatient.
It'll be a win for the ages, share some glasses, celebrate.
Gold and glitter, moments like these are partially why we begin
A New Chapter.

But it's the work we're embracing for.
That gruel I can handle, now that I have bought a lot of fuel
To throw at my fire, to cook my needs to perfection.
A new journal to put a transparent chapter in the past,
And record my thoughts as I progress along the lines as I do in life.

Because A New Chapter means the journey is unknown,
But the percentage of it being in your favor
Is worth the risk to go with it along for the ride.
No book is made from one chapter, therefore,
We go to A New Chapter.

Cowles Mountain

At sky heights, a rise so epic-
Miles so far away,
The lone Cowles Mountain greets me like a Mt. Fuji.
San Diego's transit bus ducks under bridges and scrambles around turns,
But it doesn't shake sight of that tan grand peak
With a sprinkle of Manzanitas.

My, how often I wish to meet that of which
Is within its epicenter-
An old soul that welcomes all to climb,
Challenges the ones that pursue,
And rewards the deserving for summiting.

Many will tell you there is more to a mountain than looks,
I want to rest under open skies in blueberry starlight,
On Cowles Mountain, breathing in the thin air, isolated in a nest of nature,
For one moment assuming the role of king of the mountain,
And listening to an expanse of tales it has lived through...

Ah- how mountains move me, I'll never understand.
Or how sometimes, I get the feeling
That I move mountains, too.

This Is a Journey, This Is Not a Test

Comrades, marauders, vagabonds,
This is a journey!
We're all welcome to join,
But I must confess-
The mind can mimic a field of crickets,
Chirping in unison.
The mind can mimic a field of mines,
Combusting all at once.

Nomads, wanderlust-ed, and all who are curious,
This is a test!
We're all destined somewhere,
Whether we like it or not;
Alas,
The soul in good hands finds a home with company to rest anew.
The soul in bad hands finds no home, no rest,
And tries again from learned mistakes.

Welcome Home

Home is where the heart grows fonder.
Absence spawns the seed of loneliness.
Home is the keeper of all our favorite bits & pieces.
It is everything we build around.

Home is the drive a hero needs to lift their sword against the enemy.
It is where they gallantly bring prince or princess back for safekeeping.
Home is where they call a family to be raised.
It is a place where children can call it their home.

Home can be where you can run nude up & down the stairs,
Or drink yourself stupid and not hurt anyone.
Home is the shelter from the rain and snow.
Home is a house, an apartment, a tree house, a cave, a castle.

But everyone can't be home all the time,
Nothing would get done. We'd all be indefinable inkblots on black paper.
Some move to find a new home for change,
Some go to schools far away to experience,
Some come back to a home for nostalgia,
And some homes haunt with sad memories.

But a real home is where your lungs fill with gold,
And everyday your eyes lift like the sun and moon.
You'll know in that instant, that whatever reflects your self-being,
Home can be anything, even the least suspecting.

Home can be soft grass, the dessert sand,
The sky highs, within clustered towers, deep snow,
Nestled high up in wavering evergreen pines,
Shade from bayous of Water Lilies,
The ocean.
A home can be anywhere that grants safety.
And wherever your home may be,
We all share that same feeling,
Which means you are never alone.

Dreamy Realism

Quiet cities scare citizens, so there are
Scratches upon metal grated ramps,
Echoes into the hollow subway lit by
Flick-it fluorescents.

Hidden under the Hyacinth,
The Metro passes from above and shakes the bricks.
We would sip chamomile tea and chatter about
The branches of life spreading from the tree of existence.

She took my hand and made me feel,
I forgot my heart wasn't hard as steel,
She pointed out the blueberry skies,
And I said with whipped cream,
Mother Nature and I have a genuine love appeal.

Silver Note

Who is playing that beautiful sound,
Like rain atop the roof?
I open a door, and she is the other side,
In an empty, magnolia white room,
With a great oval window that let's the light in.

Her shadow stretches in my direction,
As she watches through the glass,
Songbirds dance along telephone wires.
Her hands are at her mouth,
Playing silver notes from a harmonica in the key of G.

I glide across the room,
And humbly let my arms slide around her waist.
Our bond is unrestrictedly soul.
Ghosts of stress escape from my body,
This must be the place.

Caught in bliss, a sinless string of blue splaying lights,
Has its clever way of revealing only the most fundamental.
In the near darkness, I am radiant, playing silver notes on my guitar,
She ties bundles of foraged black sage to hang and dry.
And peace effaces the agony that used to keep me up at night.

Escaped Energy

Among the dazzling glow of midnight's moving shadows,
My heavy eyes record one last peek before deep sleep.
Her skin is soft in blue. She envelops me in her wings.
Tender in the eyes of love, precious in the hands that care,
Unforgettable to the mind that is grateful.

The silver note in the song of me.

Purpose After Purpose

Cool as ice, I am a calmer, collected self
Than I once was.
That is me, in the reflection of my black tea,
The one I always wanted to be.

Warm as condensation, I am an aware, energized self
Than I once was.
The sun, the beach, the breeze, Escaped Energy,
Even I am amazed by my presence,
From a sad, melancholy history.

In love, as wave and shore, I am a confident, determined self
Than I once was.
Higher up the ladder of life.
And I am asking the lifeguard up top,
If they have ever saved someone.

Coronado Beach

The rains of the skies sure don't know about these secret, happy places,
Where the sun's touch is gentle all day, every day.
There are constant winds that keep the ocean air fresh,
The same ones the pelicans use to take off.
The sandbar has settled in divine flakes of gold,
And when the waves meet, the water shines,

I had to cross the tallest, curviest bridge to get here.
Many jump to never make it.
I keep both hands on the wheel and look forward
To my feet in hot sand.

Darkness behind,
There is life to love here in paradise,
Where my heart soars with the pelicans,
And it's okay to cry.
It's okay to be me, unafraid, grateful,
And I thank you. Thank you, Thank you.
I am Home.